Praise for *Emissary*

"Readers of inspirational fantasy will enjoy [Bunn's] foray into a new genre."

—*Publishers Weekly*

"Book one of the Legends of the Realm series is a wonderful journey away from the real world. . . . A fine start to this intriguing series."

—*RT Book Reviews*, 4 stars

"*Emissary* is a superbly crafted fantasy adventure novel that engages the reader's total and rewarded attention from beginning to end."

—The Midwest Book Review

Praise for *Merchant*

"The reader is draw d, in the end, left eager to se ourney continues in the next

—*RT Book Reviews*

"The second Legends of the Realm book doesn't disappoint! With love, loss, and adventure, Locke has another hit on his hands."

—*Life Is Story* blog

"A deftly crafted and highly entertaining fantasy action/adventure novel from beginning to end."

—The Midwest Book Review

Books by Thomas Locke

LEGENDS OF THE REALM

Emissary

Merchant of Alyss

The Golden Vial

FAULT LINES

Fault Lines

Trial Run

Flash Point

RECRUITS

Recruits

Renegades

LEGENDS OF THE REALM • BOOK 3

THE GOLDEN VIAL

THOMAS LOCKE

Revell
a division of Baker Publishing Group
Grand Rapids, Michigan

Published by Revell
a division of Baker Publishing Group
PO Box 6287, Grand Rapids, MI 49516-6287
www.revellbooks.com

Printed in the United States of America

Library of Congress Cataloging-in-Publication Data
Names: Locke, Thomas, 1952, author.
Title: The golden vial / Thomas Locke.
Description: Grand Rapids, MI : Revell, [2018] | Series: Legends of the realm ; #3
Identifiers: LCCN 2017044958 | ISBN 9780800723873 (pbk. : alk. paper)
Subjects: LCSH: Magic—Fiction. | GSAFD: Fantasy fiction.
Classification: LCC PS3552.U4718 G67 2018 | DDC 813/.54—dc23
LC record available at https://lccn.loc.gov/2017044958

18 19 20 21 22 23 24 7 6 5 4 3 2 1

This book is dedicated to

Dr. Pei Lun Zhang

A dear friend and gifted healer

Seubral
Port Royal
Galwyn
Hil
Mineral Springs
Great
Fores
Honor
Havering
River Havering
Port Sutton
The
Hea
The Realm

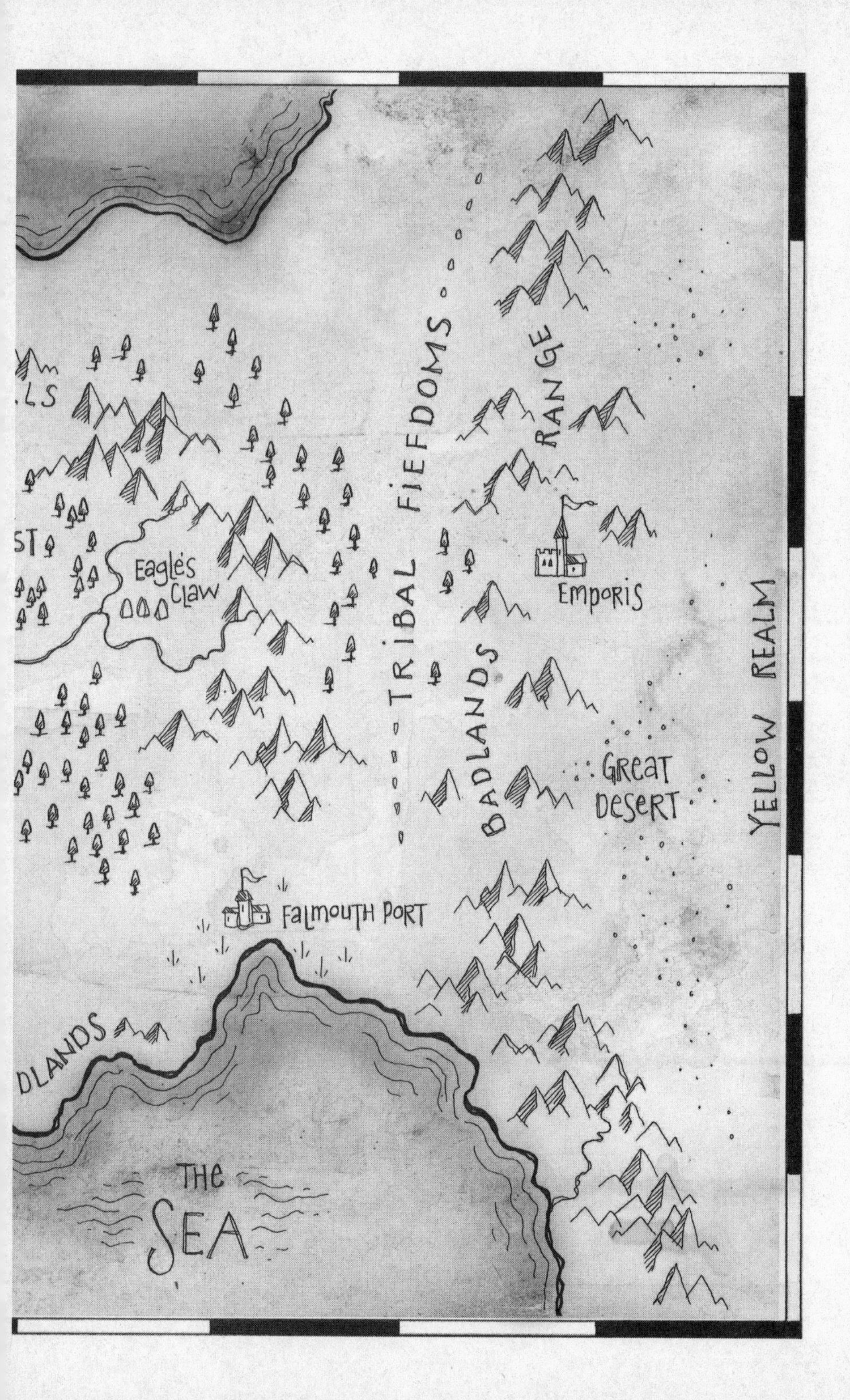

TRIBAL FIEFDOMS
RANGE
Eagle's Claw
Emporis
BADLANDS
Great Desert
YELLOW REALM
Falmouth Port
THE SEA

1

Almost everyone in the village of Honor called Dally a fortunate young woman. She had, after all, survived the fire that had robbed her of home and parents and three brothers. For years Dally heard her family's cries echo through her darkest dreams. But she had not known that nightmare for over a month now. Not since the woman had started visiting her in the night.

These new experiences were no mere dreams. Dally had known from the very first moment that the woman was real, and her name was Shona.

What was more, Shona was coming for her.

Dally was three days shy of her eighteenth birthday. Which meant she was a full year away from an end to Norvin's guardianship. Not that she minded working in the mayor's kitchen. Serving under his wife Krim, however, was another matter entirely. The big-boned woman had managed to run off every serving girl they'd employed. No family in the Three

Valleys would allow their daughter to come work in this house. Dally did not know how she could endure another month with Krim, much less a year.

Krim had not always been so. When Dally had first arrived, the mayor's wife had been gruff and stern, yet loving in her own manner. But Krim had steadily become intolerable, driven to grim harshness by the shadows that now surrounded the Three Valleys. The problem was, Dally had no living relative and no money and nowhere else to go. Their region had been sealed off from the rest of the world for almost two years now. Not even news was getting through anymore. Dally had once considered the Three Valleys to be the finest place on earth. Now it was simply a cage.

Krim's screech rang through the kitchen window. "Scamp! Wastrel! Where are you hiding! There are cows to milk and butter to churn, and I'll not be feeding any urchin who sneaks from her chores!"

Dally crouched behind the pen holding the newest litter of wolfhounds. Norvin loved the dogs and treated them like his children. Krim tolerated them because they brought in more gold than the mayor's crops, though Norvin's fields were some of the finest in the Three Valleys region. The wolfhounds had always been fiercely loyal to Dally, minding her long before they learned Norvin's commands. Dally's ability to communicate with them had grown steadily over the four and a half years she had lived in what once had served as Krim's garden shed.

Norvin claimed this particular litter was the finest he had ever raised, for all eight of the dogs possessed a white streak from snout to tail. It was said their silver fur indicated strength and loyalty and intelligence. All Dally could say for certain was, her secret bond had never been as strong as with this litter. But the dogs were fully grown now, waist high and trained and ready to be sold. Dally's heart cracked every time she thought of losing her most precious friends.

She tucked herself into the shadowed corner where the pen met the garden wall, shut her eyes, and looked through the dogs' eyes. She watched Krim shout and stomp about the yard, then retreat into the house, where she banged pots and yelled at the walls. These days, Krim was never happier than when she could scourge someone with her tongue.

Using her secret gift, Dally reached for the wolfhound whose power of smell was strongest, and sniffed the air. The dogs had a particular way of testing for distant odors. They did not inhale like humans. Instead, they sniffed once, twice, three times, tucking the wind into various pouches behind their nostrils and inside their cheeks.

There. Norvin was in the village hall. Honor's mayor was with elders who often visited their home and spent time with the dogs. Others, though, carried scents she had never known before. Which meant this particular gathering was of leaders from the entire Three Valleys. Dally quailed at the prospect of interrupting such a meeting. But she had no choice.

She checked once more to be certain Krim was turned away from the kitchen window. Then, quick as a flash, she rose and scaled the wall.

Dally scampered up the village's central lane. The adults of Honor might call her fortunate, but many village children picked on her mercilessly. To her dismay, she saw the three young girls who considered her the ideal target point in her direction, and knew they'd be off to tell Krim where she was. Which only made her run faster still.

When she arrived at the village hall, the reins of three dozen horses were tied to the front posts. From within the hall, voices rose in strident anger or fear or worry, or all three.

Then from far down the lane rose Krim's furious screech. "*Dally!* You will come here *now!*"

She wished she had thought to rebraid her hair while hiding behind the dogs' pen. Now it was too late. She licked her hands and pulled the wayward strands from her forehead. She straightened her dress but did not bother to dust herself off. Dirt caked her legs up to her knees. A bit of dust on her dress would hardly be noticed.

She took a deep breath and climbed the three front stairs.

"Dally! Girl, you better—"

Dally knocked once, loud as she could. Then she opened the door and stepped inside.

The council members were seated in a circle. Norvin frowned at the interruption and said, "Dally, this is not—"

"I have a message for you and everyone else who is gathered here," she declared.

Norvin had formerly been a cheerful man, full of great good humor. Even with all his valley now faced, Norvin's manner remained as gentle as his wife's was strident. But there were many reasons for Honor's leader to fret these days, and few occasions to smile. The creases on his face were new and deep. "Lass, it must wait—"

"An army is coming," Dally announced. "Led by a lady."

Krim's footsteps thundered up the stairs and she powered into the room. She was a heavyset woman who nowadays barreled her way through any opposition. But whatever she was about to say was halted by the sight of every elder in the hall standing and gaping at the girl by the entrance.

Dally went on, "The lady asks for the use of the fields bordering the river. She knows this will ruin your crops, and she is willing to pay."

One of the strangers demanded, "Is this some form of jest?"

"Dally has been with us since her family died in a fire over four years back," Norvin replied. "Not once in all this time have I ever known her to joke about anything."

The oldest member of their clan demanded, "How do you know of this woman?"

"We've been speaking together for over a month now," Dally replied.

Krim demanded, "And precisely why am I only hearing about this now?"

"Krim," her husband said.

"Well, I ask you, husband—"

"Krim." When his wife went silent, Norvin asked, "She comes in dreams?"

"Not really dreams," Dally replied. "She comes just before dawn, and we talk, and then she leaves."

"A witch," one of the strangers muttered.

"A queen," Dally corrected. "Her name is Shona."

The oldest of the women seated in the circle gasped.

Norvin demanded, "What is it?"

"Yagel often spoke of this one."

"The forest tinker?" A greybeard snorted. "Not to me he didn't."

"Because you called him addled and wouldn't offer the man a tin of cold water, much less listen to his news. You've been doing your best to stay blind to everything that's been happening." The woman turned back to Norvin and continued, "When the shadow-beasts began closing in—"

"We don't speak of them here," the greybeard said sharply.

"And it's because we pretend they're not out there that we've lost contact with the realm! We must do battle against the fiends, I say!"

"Elders, please." Norvin gestured for calm. He asked the old lady, "So the tinker spoke of this woman?"

"Queen Shona, the first of her name," the woman said. "Crowned by Bayard, the last of the Oberons. He knelt before her, offered fealty, and renounced any claim to the throne."

"Bayard's over in Falmouth Port," the greybeard replied. But his earlier derision was gone now, lost to the curiousness of a young woman speaking of news from distant lands. "All the way over by the badlands."

"And yet Dally here claims an army has crossed the realm and is coming to Three Valleys," Norvin said. He studied Dally, then asked, "So this lady comes to you in the night and speaks with you."

"Clear as you and me." Dally hesitated, then decided they needed to hear the rest. "Except for today. This time she spoke while I was feeding the dogs."

"What, just now?"

"That's why I burst in like I did. I was to deliver you an urgent message. The lady knows of our troubles and she will offer us help. She says to tell you she can't promise to make all our problems vanish. But she can make things better than they are now. And she will do her best to keep us safe."

The valley's elders pondered for a time, then Norvin asked, "Was there anything else, lass?"

"Just one thing," Dally replied. "She arrives at dawn."

2

Dally was lithe and slender with lovely hands that had been scarred and roughened with hard work. Her most beautiful feature was her hair, which held to a shade of permanent autumn. It was brown and red and gold all at the same time, long and silky and thick as a living rope. Her eyes were green and held such intensity many people actually turned away.

Most folks could not say precisely what it was that caused them to flinch under her gaze. But something burned inside those eyes that frightened all but the smallest and least of the villagers. The children loved her. Animals vied for her attention. Ever since childhood, Dally could milk the most ill-tempered cow and never know a scratch or a kick. The most savage of village curs crouched low to the earth and whined, begging for her touch.

But for most of her village, especially those of her own age, Dally's gaze was deeply unsettling.

Even the young men who thought they might have their sweet way with the lovely kitchen wench retreated from those eyes. Why precisely, they could not say, or would not. Perhaps they feared Dally saw to the secret core of their dark lusts. As a result, most young men shunned her. The women her age mocked and taunted her. And afterward, when they gathered together and struggled to excuse their actions against one so defenseless, they resorted to the word their parents used to describe Dally.

Strange.

As a result, Dally grew up isolated and hurting and alone. And something else besides.

The mayor's household did not own a mirror, as was the case with many hidebound families. Back in the dark days, so long ago that even the legends had been forgotten, it was said that certain witches could treat mirrors as portals and reach through and capture those who studied their reflection.

So Dally had only the other young people's attitudes to gauge how she looked. And from their response, she had no choice but to assume that she was ugly as well as alone.

At dawn the next day, the night guards rushed into the village. But they did not announce that soldiers were approaching. For Shona's army was already there.

A place centrally located yet set apart. A location they could easily fortify. A habitat within clearly defined boundaries that they could claim as their own. Even before Shona had finished her request, Dally already knew the answer. She had told the young queen where to go. And by the time the sun was fully over the horizon, it appeared as though the camp had been there for years.

Even so, no citizen of the Three Valleys met this so-called queen for nearly a month. For most of that period, Dally remained the only line of communication between the Three Valleys inhabitants and the newcomers.

There were several hundred in the army, perhaps more. Every three or four days Dally was informed of their immediate needs—so much bread and meat, vegetables of this or that type, horses needing a shoe or suffering from a saddle sore. The land occupied by the army extended into the river like a huge thumb and was rimmed on three sides by the streaming water. The stone dike that kept the spring floodwaters at bay had been laid in place by Norvin's great-great-grandfather. Even when the newcomers fashioned a thorn barrier from the forest perimeter and sealed off the entire peninsula for their use, Norvin did not complain.

But after sixteen days, and the deliveries of food and supplies continued to mount, and still there had been no word emerging from the camp, Krim began urging her husband to demand payment.

Another four days passed, and Dally could hear Krim's complaints echo through every window of their home. She knew she was at least partly at fault for Krim's rising anger. The entire village watched Dally now. Krim's harsh rule over her life had ended, at least temporarily. Even so, Dally still ate her meals on the stoop of the shed. She tended the vegetable garden and she washed the cottage floors and she milked their cows and she helped Norvin with the dogs. But much of her time was spent on the river's edge, staring at the camp and wondering if the queen might ever again wish to visit in the night with a lowly kitchen girl.

Now and then she thought perhaps she caught a glimpse of the queen walking around the enclosure. Dally never saw the woman's face, of course. But the cloak she wore was of some remarkable weave. Leggings of some golden material peeked from the cloak's lower rim. What was more, the hood was lined in a strip of royal purple. And everyone the lady passed either saluted or bowed or both. If the woman responded in any form, Dally never saw.

The first direct contact between Honor and the newcomers came on the twenty-third dawn. And only because Dally begged the queen to keep her best friends from being scattered throughout the Three Valleys.

Dally knew her village in the manner of a young woman who had lived through hard years. Yet despite the nightmarish events that had brought her here to the garden shed behind the mayor's house, with eight young dogs for her only friends, she loved her village and the valley region. Even now, when the forest sealed them away from the world and feral beasts slipped in to steal livestock and wreak havoc and fill their nights with desperate hours.

Through the four hard years, Dally had come to know all manners of silence. Now and then she could take her pups for a sunset walk along the empty river path, where the quiet safety surrounded her. These lonely hours chanted a soft melody, inviting her to open up and reveal the sorrows and the memories and yearnings that she spent most of her days ignoring.

Night silences were the worst. As a young child Dally had loved the dark hours, when the world was still and she was tucked safely into her little bed in the room under the rafters. She heard her brothers' sleep-breaths from the next room, soft as midnight tunes. She heard the quiet laughter as her parents ended another long day. She sensed the love that filled their home and the knowledge that she belonged here. Their fields were close to the forest, and Dally and her brothers had loved to play along the border, fighting pretend beasts and eating berries and dreaming of great quests to come.

Until the night that changed her world forever.

She was the only one awake when she heard the beast that the valley's occupants wanted to believe was merely a fable. A tale used to frighten misbehaving children. But Dally knew otherwise. Her worst night hours always began with the sound that beast had made. Just before the flames had enveloped her home. Now the silence contained within the dark hours was a fiend.

This morning's silence was something else entirely.

Dally was up long before the sun and quietly finished her chores before the rest of the house awoke. Since the meeting with the valley's elders, Krim had taken to suppressing her foulest moods. Even so, it was increasingly difficult to be around the woman. Dally knew sooner or later Krim would explode, releasing all the ire and invective her husband had ordered her to stifle.

The morning began like most others in a farming village, with the roosters challenging the day and farming families noisily beginning their chores long before the sun was fully up. Then Honor became enveloped by a breathless hush.

Knowing what was about to happen kept Dally tossing and turning all night. She had drawn fresh well water and washed herself by the light of the morning star. She wore her cleanest shift and her only shoes. Her long auburn hair was neatly plaited. But there was nothing she could do about the way her hands shook or the tight manner of her every breath. The dogs sensed her anxiety and whined about her legs.

Then Norvin called through the kitchen door, "Dally, could you join us?"

The way he spoke it as a request was enough to set her heart to fluttering like a caged bird. Dally let herself out and made a mess of refastening the pen's lock. Norvin was there in the doorway, his broad features creased by genuine shock. Silently he led her through the house to where Krim stood, hands tucked into her apron, transfixed by the apparition looming outside her front door.

Two warhorses called destriers were flanked by half a dozen foot soldiers outside the front gate. One rider was a woman, yet she bore the same warrior-hardened expression as the man standing beside her. Their helmets were inscribed with golden crowns. Their mail held links of gold and silver both. They wore identical over-mantles that were sewn with the same crest Dally had seen upon the queen's robes. Their sword hilts and scabbards and belts were encrusted with precious jewels.

When Dally stepped into the daylight, the officers touched fists to chests and bowed as one.

She knew how to respond because Shona had told her, and Dally had practiced in the shed's secret confines. Ignoring the villagers who stood and gaped, she curtsied so deep her left knee touched the flagstones.

"The Lady Shona sends her greetings to the family of Dally," the woman said. "I am Meda, colonel of the palace guard. This is Captain Alembord, my second."

Dally had been told how to respond to this as well. She bowed back, but only slightly, and said, "This is Norvin, mayor of Honor, and his wife Krim."

Meda gave them both a terse nod and told Norvin, "My lady asks your pardon. She owes you both thanks and payment. But she is observing a month of mourning. The Lady Shona prefers to wait until this is ended before starting new alliances."

Norvin stammered, "Who does she mourn?"

"The one you know as Hyam," Meda replied. "He has suffered a great loss. Our lady and all her company mourn with him. Hyam's loss is a wound to us all."

Norvin's curiosity took hold of his tongue. "You said the one we know as Hyam. How else is he named?"

Meda had clearly been expecting the question. "Prince of the realm. Consul to Lady Shona. Senior wizard. Emissary."

Krim muttered, "I knew he was a secret wizard. Told you, I did."

Meda kept her gaze upon the mayor. "Secret no longer."

Norvin's mouth opened and shut several times before he said, "Our . . . Dally called Shona a queen."

"She has been crowned but does not use the title herself. And will not, until the scourge in Port Royal is destroyed and Shona assumes the throne." Meda ended the questions by saying, "Now if you will be so good as to show me your dogs."

3

Two of the foot soldiers followed them around the side of the house, apparently intending to guard their officers even in the mayor's backyard. Norvin's house fronted the nearest of his fields, with a low stone wall separating the dog pen and kitchen garden from the mayor's herd of prize cattle. Colonel Meda paused when the garden shed came into view. She stooped down, peered inside, then turned slowly and took aim at Krim. Meda's glare was enough to send the mayor's wife scooting for the back door.

Alembord drew her back around by saying, "They're the spitting image of Dama."

Norvin asked, "Who?"

"Hyam's wolfhound." Meda smiled at the dogs pressing tight against the fence. "She had the same white streak down the length of her."

"Aye, that's right. She does." Norvin smiled at the memory. "She's one of my finest. Dama, you say? Interesting name."

"It means blood ally in Elven." Meda put a hand through the fence, allowing the dogs to sniff her. "Alas, Dama is no more."

The words pushed Norvin back a step. "Elven, did you say? And Dama . . ."

"Died protecting us from . . . a fiend. I myself owe my life to one such as these." Meda turned away from the dogs and the memory both. "Our lady wishes to acquire them all."

Norvin was clearly still struggling to catch up. "But . . . I regret . . . three are claimed."

Meda did not actually grip her sword. Instead, her hand merely dropped to rest upon the jeweled hilt. "Perhaps I did not make myself clear. The Lady Shona will purchase all eight. You need but name your price."

Norvin must have seen something in the officers' gazes, for he merely replied, "No doubt my other buyers can wait for the next litter."

"Excellent. The Lady Shona will be most grateful. The wolfhounds are now to be in the exclusive care of Lady Dally."

"In . . . Yes, yes, of course. But she's not . . ."

Meda cut off his comment by turning to Dally and saying, "I hear you have the gift of communication."

"Aye, mistress."

"You may address me as Colonel," Meda said, but not unkindly. "But my friends call me Meda."

Dally had no idea what to say, so she remained silent.

Meda pointed her chin at the dogs. "Which are you close to?"

"If you mean, which do I . . ."

"Bond with," Meda offered. "Speak to without words."

Dally gestured at the pen. "These here."

"What, *all* of them?"

"Well, the mam, she can be a bit difficult. And the sire is getting on—he sleeps much of the day. We don't really . . . But all the eight pups . . ." She stared through the gate. "They're my friends."

Meda said to the wide-eyed Norvin, "Be so good as to open the gate." When that was done, she said, "Show me."

It was easy enough, for the dogs were very attentive now. They had the unique intelligence and sensitivity of silverbacks, and so when Dally reached out, they were already prepared to accept her. She drew them over to various points around the rear garden. She reached, she smelled, she listened.

Finally she said, "You've got more troopers stationed along the main road between here and your compound. And others scouting the forest perimeter. Some of the horses are shying away from taking the paths. They smell . . ."

Meda and Alembord closed the space between them. "What do they smell?" Meda asked.

Dally released her hold and blinked as the world returned to the limited focus of human eyes. She replied, "The fiends."

4

Dally ate her midday meal with the dogs. She had no interest in entering the house. Her secret was out, which meant there was no longer any need to cage the wolfhounds. She unlatched their pen's door and allowed them to mill about in a tight circle. There was great comfort to be found in their closeness. They were massive beasts now, standing tall as her waist and weighing almost as much as she did. She directed two of them to sit down to her left, which shielded her from Krim's glare out the kitchen window.

The next astonishment arrived a few hours later. Only this time Dally was caught completely unawares.

There were regular cycles to most farming days, and these depended upon the season. Now that the spring planting was done and most of the farm animals had delivered their young, the valley was able to take a long, slow breath before harvesting began. Added to this was the fact that every able-bodied villager stood sentry one night in four. As a result, when the sun reached its zenith and the heat was stifling, the entire valley took a long, somnolent pause.

So only the restless and the young were witness to an event that was to form the fireside legends for generations to come. This was the day that the Long Hall wizards broke their oath.

For over a thousand years, all magic within the realm had been restricted to communities known as Long Halls. The Three Valleys wizards were cloistered in a walled fortress a full two days' walk from the nearest village. The trail had been cut for almost a year, and those young acolytes who had set off to join them had not been heard from again. The wizards were little more than fables now, mythic figures played by dreaming children.

Yet on this sultry afternoon, eight grey-robed mages walked down Honor's central lane.

Dally's first notice of anything amiss came by way of a soft huff from one of the wolfhounds. But before she could ask what it was, she heard a sharp rapping upon the mayor's front door. Then all the dogs went to full alert. Dally was on her feet long before the cries and running feet sounded along the front lane.

Through the open kitchen window, Dally saw Norvin adjust his suspenders before opening the door. There followed a brief conversation that Dally could not hear, and yet was enough to set her heart to pounding once again.

Then the grey-robed woman pointed through the house, beyond the kitchen window, directly at Dally.

Without waiting for Norvin's response, the woman slipped past him, crossed the threshold, ignored Krim entirely, and passed through the house and out the rear door. "Are you the one they know as Lady Dally?"

"I . . . Yes, mistress."

"Excellent." Up close the woman was both small and quite old, though her grey eyes held the sparkle of vibrant youth. "I am Edlyn. For years I served as Mistress of the hidden orb in Falmouth Port. But while I visited the Three Valleys Long Hall, the former Mistress passed on. The mages in their wisdom asked me to take her position. No doubt much to their regret." She indicated a slender bearded young man who stood three paces back. "This is Myron, my aide."

"An honor, Lady Dally."

"Time is crucial just now, young lady. Will you allow me to skip pleasantries and come straight to the point?"

Dally was tempted to say this was already the most pleasant conversation she'd had in a very long while. "Whatever you want, Mistress."

"Excellent. Will you show me your abilities with these remarkable animals?"

"Of course, ma'am."

"Make no sound nor give any signal, if you please."

Scarcely had Dally drawn the wolfhounds into position and identified the five other mages who stood by Norvin's front stoop when Edlyn said, "All right. I've seen enough." She turned to Myron and said, "Be so good as to fetch us two chairs."

The aide dropped the sack he carried, crossed the rear yard, walked past where Norvin and his wife gaped through the door, and swiftly returned with straight-back chairs from the master's table. "Will these do, Mistress?"

"Thank you. Come sit beside me, Dally. Now then. I have heard you communicate with our Lady Shona in dreams."

"Not really dreams, Mistress. They're something else entirely."

"I understand." Both mages were clearly pleased by her response. "Now I need to ask you, do you have any other dreams?"

Dally tensed. "You mean, about the forest beasts attacking my family?"

The Mistress glanced at her aide, then replied, "These are very important. But they are not for now. I am looking for something very specific. We mages require a sign, if you will. One I cannot speak of unless . . ."

"Oh. You mean the candles."

Edlyn leaned back, clearly very satisfied. "Tell me about them."

"I light one. I make the fire myself. Then the flame becomes alive."

"Wonderful." Edlyn gestured to her attendant, who untied the clasp to his sack.

Dally went on, "Then they speak to me."

Both mages froze. "I'm sorry. They speak?" Edlyn asked.

"They did. Before these dogs came. Not in words. But . . ." Dally looked from one face to the other. "Did I do something wrong?"

"Lass, let me assure you of this one thing. Whatever events that have filled you with such fear are now behind you."

Something broke within Dally. She could no more hold back the tears than stop her own breath. She covered her face with her hands and leaned down until she was settled upon her thighs.

Edlyn's hand rested upon her shoulder. "Dear child, listen carefully to what I am about to say. You are far from the first who has suffered because of their magical talent. But that time is now past."

Dally's entire being was filled with the most horrid question that had plagued her worst nights. "Did I draw the beast that killed my family?"

"If you will please straighten up and look at me, I will answer you. Thank you. Dally, I will never lie to you. Even when the truth is at its most painful, you can trust me to be both direct and honest. The answer is, your talents are so remarkable it is possible they were noticeable to our foes. But I very much doubt this. Latent powers are invisible to even our most sensitive adepts."

Dally cleared her face with trembling hands. "I miss them so."

"And it is one of the many things that makes you so precious." She gestured to her attendant. "Now let us begin."

But as her aide brought out two candles thick as Dally's arm and set them atop iron holders, Mistress Edlyn said, "Just a moment." She frowned at the rear wall, then the dogs, and declared, "This won't do at all."

Myron said, "The house, perhaps?"

"My thoughts exactly." She rose to her feet. "Wait here."

Edlyn walked to the rear door where Norvin and Krim still stood and spoke in a voice too low for Dally to hear.

Myron pointed to the wolfhound standing beside Dally's chair. "Can you tell me what the Mistress is saying?"

Dally found she did not mind his desire to observe her

abilities. The Mistress's words had opened something inside her. Dally realized the need for subterfuge was over. She stifled the upsurge of fresh tears and shut her eyes.

Through the dog closest to the house, Dally heard Krim say, "And I'm saying this is my house. I don't have to give it up for no one."

Norvin merely sighed.

"That is most certainly correct," the Mistress replied. "But think on this. In times to come, when legends speak of this very hour, how do you wish to be known? As the woman who treated a young mage as your kitchen slave?"

Krim bridled. "I'll have you know—"

"I'm not done." The steel in Edlyn's voice stifled Krim's unfinished protest. "Instead, you might care to do us this favor and thus be known as a woman who did what was best for the realm."

Dally opened her eyes and said, "Mistress Edlyn is having words with the mayor's wife."

"Good." Myron slipped into the chair beside Dally. "It is remarkable, this ability of yours to bond. And do so without any formal training."

Dally had no idea how to respond. She remained silent.

"Nor do I recall seeing Mistress Edlyn so excited."

"She appears so calm."

"It is her way of leading. By being the eye of the storm." He studied the wolfhound poised by Dally's side. "Do they mind you pushing them aside?"

Dally understood his question and replied, "I don't take their place. I join in beside them. I'm their friend."

The Mistress turned and beckoned. "Let's move inside, you two."

Myron gathered up his candles and sack. As he passed Mistress Edlyn, Myron declared, "We have so much to learn from this one."

Edlyn told Dally, "You know what I want you to do, yes? From your dreams."

"I think . . ."

"Tell me."

The mayor's wife must have sighed or muttered or shifted, for the mage turned and said, "This is your final caution. Utter a sound or shift one iota, and I will freeze you so tight your very breath becomes a battle."

To his credit, Norvin protested, "There's no call for such threats."

"See that there is not." Edlyn turned back to Dally, gathered herself, and repeated, "You know what I want you to do."

They were seated at the dining table. Norvin and his wife were restricted to the corridor leading to their bedchamber. Through the front window Dally could see three other mages standing sentry along the front wall, holding the gawping villagers at bay. Two more stood just inside the doorway, there to serve as witnesses.

What Dally found most remarkable was how the Mistress had not asked if she was able to perform this deed. Instead, Edlyn had stated it as fact.

Dally softly murmured, "I am to reach . . ."

"Remember what I said earlier," Mistress Edlyn said. "The time for fear and secrecy and whispers is over. Now I want you to sit up straight. That's better. Take a deep breath. Another. Now I want you to see your next words as a declaration. Your life is about to take a new turning. Ready? All right. Now tell me and the entire world who you are."

Dally had to pause long enough to wipe her cheeks. "I light one candle, then I pass the flame to the other."

"Correct. And after that?"

"I . . . I am to bond with the fire."

"Excellent. The proper term is, you *claim* the force. Young lady, this statement alone sets you apart. Most acolytes must have their dream interpreted. The candle speaks to them, but they do not understand what is required."

Dally resisted the urge to duck her head once more. "Am I what you said? An acolyte?"

"Of that I am certain. Now light the candles and declare as much to all the mages of this world."

Dally had known she could connect with the invisible forces ever since her very first month serving in the mayor's house. It was one of the elements that had helped her survive this long, as she could draw the candle's force around her and thus remain shielded from the home's tension. This same act of shielding had also offered insight into how the mayor's wife had gradually changed from a cross woman into a bully. It was Krim's way of handling the dread that dominated the entire valley. Dally could feel Krim's hostility radiating through the house. But she also knew that her time of fearing this woman was over.

As though to confirm this realization, Dally drew upon the power. And forged a flame in the center of her palm.

This time, the Mistress did not snap at Norvin and Krim when they both gasped. Dally was not sure Edlyn even heard them. In the most frigid nights, when her little shed had been sheathed in winter's ice, Dally had lit the flame and been comforted in so many ways. Such instances were the only times when she permitted herself to recall earlier fires and the family who had nestled about it, sharing comfort and safety.

The thought of perhaps having a new place she could call home was distracting enough to dim her vision. But only for a moment.

Dally lit the first candle. She allowed it to burn for a moment, then plucked the flame from the wick and lit the second. Just as in her dream.

Only now, at this crucial juncture, two things happened that she had never foreseen.

First, Myron said quietly, "As smooth a transfer as ever I have seen. Bravo."

And second, the Mistress said, "I think we should shift the focus of our next test."

Her aide said, "I absolutely agree."

"My dear, we require a sign that you are capable of controlling the force. I want you to tell me how the candle speaks with you."

"I ask a question."

"What kind of question?"

"Most any kind. I ask, the flame takes me." It was just

the two of them now. All the others who leaned forward and listened intently, the massed villagers outside her window—they were merely shadows painted against the backdrop of her former existence. "Usually I ask what life is like somewhere else."

"You are shown the answer, is that what you are saying?"

"The answer, the place, the people, it's all the same. I ask, I see."

Edlyn nodded slowly. "It is called far-seeing, and it is a rare feat indeed. Can you look into the future or the past?"

"Neither. Only the now. I've tried to see the past, but I . . ."

"Tell me."

"I asked to see my family. The answer was a wall. Dark and hard as death." Dally flushed. "The same wall blocked me when I asked if I would know a lover in the future. But sometimes, not often, I've been shown events that lead up to the answer I seek."

Edlyn continued to nod in time to Dally's words. "So the portal only opens when you ask the proper question. Very well. I wish to ask about events that impact this day and place. Let us see if it is possible for you to apply this gift to the needs of others. Are you ready?"

"I . . . Yes. But I haven't spoken with the flame in well over a year."

"So let us see if the force is still yours to claim." Edlyn leaned in closer. "What has happened to our dearest friend Hyam, as a result of the events of . . ."

Her aide softly supplied, "Twenty-nine."

"Twenty-nine days ago," Edlyn said. "If you are allowed,

tell us where he was just before then. And what happened that led to where he is now, and what he still endures."

Dally reached out and drew the lit candle closer toward her. She took a long, slow breath, gathering herself, drawing away from all that surrounded her. Then she asked the question.

And she went.

5

She saw.

The candle's flame opened and enveloped her. The next thing she knew, Dally observed an entire city fashioned from stone as dark as slate, with a massive castle at its heart. And yet despite the forbidding color, Dally knew this was a haven against all the forces that threatened their realm.

She saw.

A gathering of many races. Elves and Ashanta and men. Dally did not know of their existence until then, and yet now she could name the individuals. Kings and queens and leaders, all. Chieftains of the badland clans. All united against the forces that sought to enslave mankind.

She could name those as well now. The Milantians. The race of wizards, defeated ten centuries past, now on the rise once more.

Dally watched them crown Shona, saw her take the oath to lead them in the battle to come.

Then she realized with a start that Shona was scarcely older than she was herself. And yet there was something about how Shona wore the mantle of power that made her age of no importance.

Then Dally realized Shona was a mage as well. A warrior queen with the wizard forces at her command.

Dally saw how this gathering broke the treaties of a thousand years and realized that it was intended as an affirmation of the need for change.

She realized this was also why Mistress Edlyn and her accompanying wizards had entered Dally's village. Because the treaties had been revoked by the same urgent needs of this new age.

She saw.

After the ceremony, Dally watched as Hyam returned to the Elves' hidden realm. The Elves kept four guards on formal duty by the secret forest portal, waiting for him.

Hyam came to a tree that served as home and sickroom both. He climbed a living staircase and entered a balcony, where his wife Joelle lay.

Dally knew in the mysterious gift of the candle's awareness that Joelle's life breath had been stolen by a Milantian mage. The mage had been destroyed, but Joelle remained trapped within this coma. There was nothing the healers could do. She slept and did not dream, scarcely breathing, held to this earth by the slightest of physical bonds. And by Hyam's love.

The scene shifted, and though the two figures remained exactly as they had been, Dally realized time had passed. Far too much time. A year and a half by human count, though here in the green kingdom time did not possess the same relentless grip. Hyam had come and gone several times, traveling far and battling his way through several skirmishes. Then returning. To this place.

Twenty-nine days before this one, Joelle's nursemaids murmured soft greetings and departed. Hyam knelt by her side so as to fit his face close to hers. When that was not enough, he burrowed into the warm softness where her hair fell over his face, cutting off his connection to anything beyond his bond to Joelle. He breathed in the warmth and tasted her skin. The Elves had used some flowered fragrance when they washed her, and it tingled softly on his lips. But it was still her, the unique beauty still there, even when her breath came so softly he feared it had stopped altogether.

Then Dally heard, "Hyam."

Hyam lifted his head. Joelle was watching him. "Beloved, are you . . ."

Her shush was soft as the dusk. "Listen to me. I am departing."

"Joelle, no, you mustn't, you can't—"

Again the shush, gentle as a first kiss. "Hyam, you must live for us both."

And she was gone.

She saw.

They buried Joelle as they would an Elven queen. The last remaining king of the Elves, Darwain, and his wife served as Hyam's seconds. The regents of the hidden realm sang a lilting dirge to the tree that had sheltered Hyam's beloved. Then the queen turned to Hyam and declared that her friend the tree would be honored to serve as Joelle's pyre.

Hyam spoke the required words, though Dally knew it almost wrenched his own life from his body. "Let it be done."

As the sun rose over the emerald kingdom, Darwain and his wife chanted words that resonated deeply. Joelle remained where she had breathed her last, upon the balcony, so high above them she might already have ascended partway to heaven.

Then the Elven rulers went silent, and the tree burst into flames.

Though the funeral party ringed the tree's base, they felt nothing, for all fire was directed upward, as fierce a power as it was silent, carrying Joelle aloft on her final earthly voyage.

Dally watched as ashes were gathered in three urns. Hyam intended to spread the contents of his urn around the garden Joelle had planted, the one surrounding their home within the magical grove. The second urn was accepted by the senior wizard of Falmouth Port, a greybeard named Trace. Dally knew he intended to burn it with the collective mage-force of every Falmouth wizard. The third was to be transported to the Ashanta territory from which Joelle had been banished. For Hyam's wife had been a forbidden mix of human and Ashanta blood. Her exclusion had been overturned by the coming of a new age. And now Joelle's remains would be planted by the Eagle's Claw offering stone, granting her a permanent resting place in the land from which she had been expelled.

The procession wound through the woodlands, back to the palace at the lake's heart. There Darwain and his queen made all welcome. The minstrels sang, and the company of men and Ashanta and Elves knew the peace of shared sorrow. And the company struggled for a means to show Hyam that he was not alone. That he was, in fact, a friend to all.

6

The secret kingdom receded until all Dally saw was the candle's flame. She straightened, eased the tension in her neck, took a long breath, and looked around.

Dally had not been aware until that moment that she had spoken at all. But she must have, for she saw that both Edlyn's and Myron's faces were streaked with tears. The mages by the front door wept openly.

Mistress Edlyn wiped her eyes with the hem of her robe. She rose slowly to her feet and addressed the dumbfounded couple still hovering in the side corridor. "The Lady Shona wishes to meet with the leaders of Three Valleys. She invites three elders from each village to gather with her in two days."

Norvin seemed to have difficulty finding his voice. "But that isn't enough time to alert the farthest villagers."

"Riders have already been sent." Edlyn turned and offered Dally a tremulous smile. "My dear, be so good as to walk out with me."

The sunlight seemed to pierce Dally, as if the experience had left her hold on life very tenuous indeed.

Edlyn slowed her step to match Dally's uncertain movements and said, "Do you understand why Shona has not greeted you personally?"

"Meda said she is in mourning."

"Joelle was her dear friend. She carries the sorrow we all feel, and more."

"Mistress, I don't understand why you feel it necessary to explain such things to me."

Myron stood by the open gate and smiled back at the two of them.

Edlyn said, "I like you, Dally. Your gifts extend far beyond the abilities with magic."

"No one has called me such as that before. Gifted."

"I told you, those times are over." Edlyn stopped her midway down the path and lowered her voice so that it would not carry to the throng watching them from the lane. "To answer your question, the gift you have demonstrated is quite rare. Especially among humans. What is more, as I listened to you just now, I was filled with a certainty that you shall play a vital role in the conflict to come."

Dally turned her back to the villagers, which meant facing Norvin and Krim standing in the doorway. Her head spun with questions. She settled on, "Conflict?"

"The fiends that attacked your home, the isolation of your valley, Joelle's death, all these and many other events are tied to a greater darkness. One we have sworn to combat."

"I want to help."

"Then so you shall. A bevy of troops are going after the forest fiends tomorrow. We would like to offer a first defeat of the valley's enemy to the elders' gathering."

Dally's heart rate quickened. "When do your soldiers leave?"

"Mid-morning. Our patrols have spotted watchers from beyond the thorns at that time of day."

"Oh please, Mistress, can I come?"

"Most certainly." Edlyn started away, then added, "Be sure to bring your friends."

Dally found herself exhausted by the day's events. She slipped inside her little shed and was instantly asleep. When she awoke, night blanketed the village. She emerged to discover one of the kitchen chairs stationed by her doorway and a plate of food nestled under a checkered napkin. She ate by moonlight, feeding the occasional scrap to the dogs as they drifted about.

Candles still burned inside the mayor's house, so when she was done, Dally rose and carried the plate inside. "Thank you, mistress."

Krim's only response was to take Dally's plate and dunk it in the washing-up water.

Norvin said, "I expect you'll be leaving us soon."

"They've not said anything about the exact timing. But perhaps . . ."

"You've been a good lass, and we'll miss having you around. Won't we, Krim?"

When his wife held to her taut silence, Dally wished them both a good night and slipped out the back.

Her dreams were of fires and Elves and telepathic beings who took solemn note as she drifted in and out of their forbidden realms.

The next morning Dally was up and ready long before dawn. As she washed and then tended the dogs, she knew her world was about to undergo another drastic shift. What exactly, she had no idea. She was impatient to take the next step, and yet calmly so. She knew a remarkable sense of acceptance over how many elements of her new life were beyond her control and always would be. Which had been her situation for years. Even so, the differences were staggering.

The dogs alerted her long before the horses drummed their way up the village lane. This time Dally was by the front gate to greet them. Six soldiers rode toward her, led by Alembord. The finery the soldiers had worn on their previous day was gone now. They all wore a similar earth-colored uniform of some heavy weave. Their weapons glinted and rattled as they approached. They were accompanied by the Long Hall Mistress in a grey robe rimmed by a stripe of palest blue. One of the soldiers led a riderless horse by its reins.

Dally did her best to ignore the villagers who gaped from the lane's other side and dropped into a deep curtsy. "Greetings, Captain, Mistress. Can I offer you and your troops fresh-drawn water?"

"Thank you, lady. But the outriders are already in position." Alembord's grim intent matched his armaments. He untied a leather satchel from his saddle horn and offered it to her. "You need to don these."

The satchel's leather was supple as felt and was sealed by a buckle of solid silver. "You want . . ."

Mistress Edlyn said, "It is the uniform of warrior mages and their acolytes. You are going into combat. You need to be properly clothed."

"I would ask that you hurry, my lady," Alembord said. "The colonel does not like to be kept waiting."

7

Dally scurried back to her shed and unsealed the satchel. She forced herself to move faster than she would have liked, for everything she saw spoke of new beginnings. The clothes were secondhand, and the alterations were hasty and in places incomplete. The leggings stretched somewhat, which was good, because they were too tight. They were colored a grey several shades darker than the mages' robes. Thin stripes of black leather ran down the outside of both legs. A singlet was worn on top, a much paler grey with a hint of blue, like a cloud before sunrise. Over this went a black leather vest with six ties and a seal embroidered over her rapidly pounding heart. Dally cinched the vest, then slipped into boots that ran almost to her knees.

She wished she owned a mirror.

When she walked back around the house, Krim offered her open-mouthed astonishment.

Edlyn said approvingly, "Now you look the part."

"All that's missing is your blade," Alembord said.

Norvin took that as his cue. "I have one she can—"

"That is kind of you, Mayor. But there is no need." Alembord handed Dally an embossed belt with scabbard and slender rapier. "Meda asked me to give you this. She says to tell you she trained with this blade, and she hopes it serves you well."

Edlyn granted her only a moment to regain control, then said, "Summon your friends, my dear. There is not a moment to lose."

Dally left Honor atop as fine a horse as she had ever seen. On one side rode the captain of Shona's palace guard. One wolfhound trotted ahead of them, another just beyond Alembord's mount. The other six made a silver-backed line behind the last troop. On Dally's other side rode the Mistress of the Three Valleys Long Hall. The entire village came out to watch the procession. As they passed the girls who had taken such pleasure in tormenting her, Dally released a long sigh.

Alembord patted his horse's flank and asked, "Can you bond with these animals as well?"

"Not in the same way as the dogs." Dally stroked the horse's mane. "I can make contact. In a small way. Sort of like saying hello."

"Do they respond?"

"Not like my wolfhounds, no. Impressions now and then." Dally straightened in the saddle. "This one knows I have only ridden a few times and promises to be gentle with me."

The main trail followed the river at the valley's heart. A narrower route ran a dozen or so paces in from the encroaching forest. Nowadays this was referred to as the guard's path. Every season the forest moved that much closer, tightening its grip. All the former trails leading into the woods were lost now, devoured by the thornbushes that formed an impenetrable wall.

Mistress Edlyn asked, "Do you know what your real name is, child?"

"My . . . I've been called Dally all my life long."

Edlyn shook her head. "I suspect your full name might well be Dahlrin."

There was a spark of memory, sharp and swift as lightning. Dally recalled her father's smiling face as he leaned over her bed and whispered the name as he lifted her to his shoulder. Then again as her little hand pulled at his whiskers. Dahlrin.

Edlyn found something in her silence that caused her to smile. "Dahlrin is not a name at all. It is an ancient title, one granted to senior wizards in the time of our war against the Milantians. It means star-fire, and signifies one whose force defies the normal standards of magery."

Dally had no idea what to say to that.

Edlyn nodded as though Dally's silence was the correct response. "Do you know your family's heritage?"

"My mam and pa were valley born and bred, Mistress. We're coming up on the boundaries of our fields." Dally pointed to a low rise on the meadow's other side. The blackened ruins were almost lost to weeds. "That's where our house stood."

Edlyn peered at the vanishing ruins, her smile gone now. As they rode on, she said, "Perhaps we should leave the mystery over your naming for another, safer time."

The watchers' trail shifted close enough to the forest barrier for Dally to see the individual thorns, some of them long as her forearm. It was the nearest she had come since the fire. She felt her fear surge with her rage at the thought of what might be lurking unseen beyond the green wall.

They approached a gently sloping rise, where soldiers awaited them. A concave slope stretched out on the hill's other side, where the main troop was stationed. They were split into nine squads of nine, each with a fighter dressed the same as Dally at their center. They seemed to Dally a small and insignificant force against the forest's silent might. A muscle beneath her rib cage began to quiver. She pressed a fist to her gut, willing it to stop. But the tremors continued to shake her middle.

She asked, "Mistress, how did you and your mages travel through the barrier?"

"There are certain questions which must wait for another time. I will answer you, but not just now." The response carried an easy assurance, as though they strolled through a flower-strewn garden. Edlyn pointed at the wolfhounds stretched out to either side of their company. "It would be good if you could select one of these to be your companion. Once this is over and we return to our temporary keep, all the other wolfhounds will need to be housed in the camp's main kennels."

"Yes, Mistress."

Alembord asked, "Will they mind being moved and then separated from you?"

"I don't know."

Edlyn asked, "Do you have a favorite?"

"These two," Dally replied, and pointed to the dogs that trotted just ahead. "The male is Nabu. He spoke to me in a dream as we ran together. It was the only time it ever happened."

Edlyn's eyes widened. "Another astonishment. Child, Nabu was the name of the lone Elven ruler who survived the Milantian wars. He founded the secret kingdom that shelters them still today. Nabu the Great."

Alembord asked, "Will the Elves mind a wolfhound taking his name?"

"It is possible." She explained to Dally, "When a ruler dies, the name is buried with them, never to be used again."

Alembord said, "And the other wolfhound you've named?"

"The female is Dama," she replied. "She's meant for Hyam. If he'll have her."

Everyone within hearing range wore a shocked expression. Finally Alembord asked, "Another dream?"

"In a way, I suppose. It came to me as I returned from the candle."

Alembord asked, "Candle?"

"That too must wait," Edlyn said. "Go on, my dear."

"I sensed that Hyam is wounded. And very lonely." Dally felt foolish sharing such impressions with this company. She finished, "He needs a friend."

Edlyn merely replied, “You know what that’s like, don’t you, needing a friend.”

Dally did not know how to respond.

Alembord asked, “You don’t mind losing one of your dogs?”

“She would be losing nothing,” Edlyn replied. She smiled at Dally. “You have a good heart, young lady. It will take you far.”

8

The troopers carried a weapon that Alembord identified by calling for his own halberd. The long spears were topped with blades and axes both. Between the squads and the forest lolled several dozen hounds, with as huge a man as Dally had ever seen at their center. He wore a black leather skullcap and a black vest of some pelt over leather trousers and boots that would have comfortably fit a giant.

He stomped across the ground at their approach, a huge grin splitting his dark beard. "Would you look at these beauties." He clumped a fist to his chest without taking his eyes off Dally's wolfhounds. "I didn't believe it when they told me. Wishful thinking, I said."

Alembord said, "Dally, meet Bear, master of the queen's hounds."

"Will these beasts of yours be making trouble among my lot, missy?"

"I will see that they behave," she said.

"Then you and this lot are welcome, I say. Welcome!" He knelt as Nabu approached him. Bear allowed the dog to give him a good sniff, then laughed heartily and threw his arms around Nabu's neck. "We'll give those fiends a right thumping!"

Colonel Meda came riding up at that moment. She slipped one boot free of her stirrup, swung off the saddle, and dropped to the earth. "The troops are deployed and ready. Best if we dismount, Mistress."

As two squaddies gathered up the reins and led the horses away, Alembord asked, "Any sign of the enemy, Master Bear?"

"The mutts have caught a whiff of the fiends now and again. But then it's gone off the wind."

Meda gestured at a line of fresh blood on her forehead. "I've gone up close enough to be scarred by those thorns and detected no movement."

Bear said to Dally, "Lass, what say you and I draw those great beasts of yours closer to the forest, see if they can detect something my own mutts have missed."

As they walked away from the officers, Dally pointed to his vest. "Is that pelt of yours off a bear?"

"A bear, you say?" His laugh was as big as the rest of him. "No, lass. It was one of them fiends we're hunting today. The first I ever took down. Not a battle I'm likely to forget."

"They took my family from me."

"Aye, that's what the grey lady said. Well, let's hope you have your first taste of revenge today." He pointed to an opening that had recently been chopped through the deadly hedge. "Night before last our scouts spotted one of the fiends making a sortie through here. There's another tunnel we've widened up ahead. We haven't spotted them since, more's the pity. Will your hounds know to hold back if they're challenged?"

Dally peered through the portal. She could smell the sweet scent of oozing sap. The gloom was thick as the intertwined branches. The odor left her feeling slightly nauseous. "I have no idea, Master Bear. They've never seen battle before."

"Well, it's high time, I say. Which of them has the most sensitive nose?"

Dally pointed to the smallest, who was already closest to the tunnel, her nostrils working. "This one."

"It's often the runt of the litter that has the heightened senses. Though you could hardly call any of this lot stunted." He pointed his chin at the opening. "Send her in."

In reply, Dally dropped to her knees and hugged the dog close, willing her to heed the call to return. Then she released the wolfhound and shut her eyes, moving in with the dog.

The forest sounds were new to them both. The odors were almost overwhelming, at least for a few moments. Somewhere in the distance Dally felt a nudge to her right shoulder, and knew in that detached manner of her bonding that Nabu had moved in close to shelter her during this time of greatest vulnerability. Then she shifted her focus back fully to where the smaller wolfhound stepped tentatively forward, one careful paw at a time. Gradually the sounds and scents began to meld into a keen awareness of this new terrain. Together they filtered out one sensation after another, until Dally could focus upon the odor that most definitely did not belong.

"Lass?"

"They're here."

In response, Bear turned and bellowed to the others. Dally heard the running footsteps, but mostly she remained intent upon the sensations beyond the thorn wall.

Meda squatted in the grass beside her. "Tell me what you've found."

"There are too many to count. They're holding back." Dally breathed in with the dog, tucking the scents into pockets and folds that were only momentarily hers to claim. "They know I'm here."

Bear said, "You mean us or the dog?"

Meda shushed him, then said, "Go on, Dally."

"Two of them are moving closer." Dally felt the lead dog's growl deep in her chest. She willed her scout to remain fast, but the temptation grew in her like a flame. Then she realized, "It's a trap!"

"Time to pull back," Bear said.

"Not yet," Meda snapped. "Describe what is happening."

The fiends were silent and swift. They spread out in a pinscher action, ready to close in from all sides. Dally willed the wolfhound to hold her ground, taking in all she could sense. She spoke in tight breaths, half-formed impressions, as the words were not easy to grasp amid all these elements of danger lust. She finished with, "The enemy is not really a forest beast at all."

"Just as we've suspected," Edlyn said.

Dally went on, "There's true animal in their blood, and something else. Something . . ."

"Magical," Meda offered quietly.

"Very dark. Very old, like a grave that's been left fallow for a time beyond time."

"All right. That's enough. Come out from there."

The dog turned and sprinted out. Dally opened her eyes. She hugged the returning scout and stared at the tunnel lined with wooden blades. A shiver coursed through both of them. Nabu nuzzled closer and licked her face.

Edlyn asked the colonel, "What are you thinking?"

"They're hoping we will attack them on their terms," Meda said. "We sent in a scout and withdrew it safely. Now they're waiting for us to move in with force."

Dally shivered once more. "She's right."

Meda slipped her knife free from its scabbard and drew a wall in the earth by her feet, thinking aloud. "So here's the enemy. Set up in formation, on their terrain. Everything's as they want it. What we need is a lure strong enough to draw them out."

Alembord offered, "They need to think we're weak enough that they can attack and retreat safely."

"Magic," Edlyn said. "Magic is the key."

"Weak magic," Meda corrected. "Something that makes them think our side isn't strong enough to handle a full-on assault."

Dally knew the answer even before Meda finished fashioning the thought. She hugged the scout more tightly still. "I'll go," she said. "Send me."

9

There followed a longish pause, as if the day itself needed to ponder Dally's offer.

At a sign from Edlyn, her aide left his position in the nearest squad and rushed over. "Mistress?" Even before Edlyn finished her explanation, Myron said, "I should be the one to go."

"I'll have the dogs to protect me," Dally said.

"Can't you send them with me as well?"

"Yes, but . . ."

Meda said, "Go on, tell us."

"The colonel said we needed to show weakness. Your aide would only be pretending. I'm . . ."

"Completely untrained," Myron finished for her. "Utterly without any combat experience."

"All she needs is one spell," Meda said. "Is that possible?"

"It is," Edlyn said.

Myron protested, "You don't know that."

"I am absolutely certain," Edlyn replied.

"Mistress . . . then why did you call me over?"

"Because I want you there in case I'm wrong."

Myron chewed on that. "I'll go. Of course. But . . ."

"This is for the best," Edlyn insisted. She reached for the leather scabbard hanging from her belt. "My dear, I want you to take my wand."

Dally accepted the device with numb fingers. The wooden handle was longer than Meda's blade and inscribed with some unknown script. The letters did not appear carved into the surface at all, but rather looked as though they had grown naturally along its length. The wand was topped by a glowing oval gemstone, held in place by a trio of slender roots.

Myron started, "Do you really think—"

"I do. Dally, slip the wand into your belt there beside your sword. That's it. Now listen carefully." Edlyn spoke a series of slow syllables, enunciating each very carefully. "Can you say that?"

A very unique sensation filled Dally. It seemed as though she had known this spell since birth, even before then. As though it was a vital component of her bones and sinew. She repeated the sounds and felt a power surge through her, rising up from the earth and causing her entire being to resonate.

"Perfect the first time," Myron said, looking astonished.

"Very good, my dear. Now this time when you say it, on the last syllable I want you to extend the hand that will be holding the wand. Hard, like you are thrusting a sword into your enemy. Ready? All right. Go."

Dally turned slightly so she faced the thorn barrier, and

did as Edlyn instructed. When she reached the final syllable, she stabbed her empty hand, willing it to carry destruction to the fiend that had destroyed her home.

Directly ahead of her, the thorns trembled slightly.

Bear said, “Did you see that?”

“A wind,” Myron said.

Meda replied, “There’s not a hint of breeze.”

Bear chuckled. “The lady’s a natural, no question.”

Edlyn nodded approval and told the group, “We are ready to proceed.”

10

As Dally moved through the thornbush tunnel, one of the wooden blades snagged her right shoulder. Perhaps she was not paying careful enough attention, as her every breath was filled with the dark unknown that awaited her. But she suspected the bushes possessed the ability to snare those who encroached upon their territory. It was hardly a glancing flick, yet still the thorn sliced through her singlet and her skin. She felt little more than a pinprick, but the blood was soon streaming down her arm. It stained her sleeve black and dripped off her fingers onto the earth.

As she passed from the tunnel into the forest, Dally debated turning around. Going back to sunlight and safety. The wolfhound to her right sniffed at the blood pooling on the earth and whined. Then again, Dally reflected, perhaps the wound would heighten her ability to play the lure.

If only she was not so afraid.

Then Myron hissed softly from behind her. The sound was enough to spur her forward.

Dally had only brought Nabu and Dama with her. These were the pair she could most trust to do exactly what she ordered. She had discarded the idea of coming in unaccompanied. The fiends had been aware of the dogs before, so they needed to sense them now.

She closed her eyes and extended herself into Nabu, long enough to be certain the shadow-beasts clustered together just beyond her field of vision. She opened her eyes and searched the distant trees, trying to detect movement, but saw nothing.

Then she had an idea.

Dally closed her eyes once more, this time reaching farther than ever before. Out to where the enemy watched. She approached them, fearful, tremulous, but doing it just the same . . .

And struck a wall as dark and forbidding as the grave.

She retreated and opened her eyes, regretting that she had failed and relieved at the same time. But her attempt had brought two new realizations.

The fiends were closer than she'd thought. They could not be seen, however, for they possessed the ability to warp the forest shadows into a cloak.

She realized something else as well. The beasts assumed they held complete dominance over this situation. She represented no real threat. The forest was now their realm. They had conquered it. She was the interloper. They sought a measure of her force, just as Meda had suspected. But not because they feared her. They wanted to know what strength was held by the soldiers beyond the thorns. They would study her assault. And then they would destroy her. And afterward defeat the soldiers. Then devour the entire valley.

The prospect of more families enduring the pain and loss that had dominated her life for these long years filled Dally with a rage so potent, all her fears simply vanished. The terror she had known was consumed like a morning mist facing the noonday sun.

Dally directed the two dogs to gather behind her. Then she drew Edlyn's wand. She did not call out the spell. She screamed the words with all her might.

The resulting blast plucked smaller saplings out by their roots. Even the tallest trees were shaken to their very foundations. The shadows hiding the beasts were obliterated. The enemy tumbled about.

The fiends were momentarily stunned by the force of her spell.

Then they tasted Dally's blood.

It had sprayed out with her spell, blown into a fine mist that now engulfed the animals' senses. Their natural fury turned to a blind and ravenous hunger.

Dally wheeled about. *"Run!"*

11

The lead beasts were almost upon them as Myron and Dally fled through the tunnel. Somewhere up ahead, Meda yelled, "Hold your fire!"

Dally emerged from the shadows at full bolt, only to be blinded by the sunlight blazing straight into her eyes. She tripped over some unseen obstacle and would have gone headlong into the dirt, but strong arms gripped her and pulled her to one side.

Alembord said, "Call your dogs! For their lives!"

"Nabu, Dama, to me!"

Alembord did not follow Myron across the field to where the squads were poised for the assault to come. Instead, he planted Dally by the thorn wall, just to the left of the trailhead.

Then the fiends burst out.

Instantly her wolfhounds bayed with their lust to join the

fray. Dally screamed, "*Hold!*" The dogs whined and panted and bayed. But they remained fast by her side.

Alembord turned to two troopers whom Dally hadn't noticed until that moment. "Guard her well!" Then he raced back toward the high mound where Meda and Edlyn stood.

At first glance the enemy looked like oversized boars. Which was how the valley naysayers could remain blind as long as they had. But so much about the beasts was exaggerated. And just plain *wrong*.

Forest boars were rarely larger than a farmer's prize pig. These were huge by comparison, most over chest-high. Their backs were creased by spines that ended in sharpened staves, as if they wore a line of daggers. Their mouths were cruelly shaped, with fangs that jutted forward with each snarl.

More telling still was the sound they made. They huffed out bone-rattling coughs from deep in their throats.

Just as they did in Dally's nightmares.

She screamed, "Flames!"

"Down!" Alembord and Meda shouted the order as one.

Edlyn shrilled, "Shields up!"

The fiends did not breathe fire. Instead, they coughed out tight balls of flame that seared the grass as they flew, so intense they momentarily outshone the sun.

The warrior mages had their shields at the ready when the barrage struck. The fireballs splintered and dripped down in brilliant cascades, leaving most squads unscathed. But the flames were magical, or so it seemed to Dally. For they demolished the shields and opened the squads to a frontal assault.

As the mages reknit their shields, a soldier who did not drop swiftly enough screamed when his arm was clipped by a fireball.

Meda roared, "Plant halberds!"

The troopers knelt and jammed the ends of their spears into the earth. Their blades glinted fierce as death in the westering sun.

"Strike!" Edlyn commanded. "Strike!"

And strike they did. The mages stood behind the line of spears and shot bolts of their own fire down into the creatures.

The bloodlust drove these fiends to blind ferocity. They scrambled around their fallen and flung themselves in a mad rush straight into the blades.

Dally had never known battle before. The dust and noise and stench made it extremely difficult to understand what was happening. Even so, she could see that the beasts threatened to overwhelm the lines. More and more of the fiends sprang through the two tunnels, a surging river of fury and flames.

Bear and his hounds saved the field that day.

The first Dally knew of his attack was a pair of whistles, loud enough to pierce the clamor. His dogs were a mangy lot, clearly not chosen for their looks. Instead, they proved to be fast, agile, silent, and extremely well trained.

"Watch!" Dally shouted to her wolfhounds. "Watch!"

Bear's animals slipped alongside the attacking beasts, lithe as dancers. Their assault seemed insignificant in the face of such ferocity. They simply nipped and danced away.

Dally did not fully understand what was happening until she heard the bones crunch.

One beast after another was sent tumbling. For each one that suffered a broken leg, three or four more were taken down.

Dally shot a quick image of instruction to her own beasts, then ordered, "Attack!"

The wolfhounds may as well have been born and bred for this very moment. Their assault was that swift.

Alembord yelled for the last supporting troops to engage, and led this assault himself. His own movements were nimble as the dogs' as he leapt forward, thrusting his sword precisely through the ribs, then jumped away before the fangs could scour his legs. The squads moved forward, the lances rose and fell in an orchestra of battle. The mages sent bolt after bolt down upon the beasts.

Gradually the screams and bellows ceased. The dust settled. The field was littered with sodden lumps, some big as the soldiers were tall, all dark as night.

It was over.

12

The silence that followed the battle was deafening.

Wizards trained as healers moved swiftly among the injured. Dally's sleeve was cut away and her wound sealed. She refused the offer of a soporific, though now that the danger had passed her arm throbbed. The wolfhounds whined and clustered as a white bandage was tied in place. No one complained about the dogs, not the medics nor the others being treated. Dally thanked the mage and forced her unsteady legs to carry her to the top of the rise, where Meda and Alembord stood with Edlyn and Myron. They asked about her arm, complimented the dogs and the role they had played, then demanded a full description of her contact with the enemy.

Edlyn took note of her pallid state and sent Myron for tea. The mug was rough clay and the brew as sweet as it was strong, and it was very strong indeed. Dally felt the strength returning to her limbs and voice as she described reaching out and making her pair of discoveries.

"That was reckless," Edlyn chided her. "Had an enemy mage been among them, we would have lost you."

"But as it was, we have learned vital lessons," Meda replied. "The enemy has weaknesses, and we must use them. Go on, lass."

It was the first time she had been addressed in such a manner. Dally flushed with the pleasure of being included among this group. She described casting the spell, and how her lifeblood was expelled and the sense that it was this that had forced the enemy to attack.

"That was fortunate indeed," Alembord said.

"No matter how wise a leader might be, good fortune must still play its role," Meda said.

Edlyn frowned at the gathering dusk and did not respond.

The healer who had treated Dally climbed the ridge with Bear.

Meda demanded, "What are our losses?"

"Eleven wounded, two seriously. One may not survive the night."

"I will visit with them shortly. What of our dogs?"

Bear's voice was made deeper with sorrow. "I lost a friend, Colonel."

"I feared as much. We mourn with you. If it's any solace, they saved many a life today."

"And turned the tide in our favor," Alembord added.

Meda waved over a young scout and ordered, "Ride ahead and inform the Lady Shona of our victory. Alembord, let's you and I speak with the wounded."

The two officers made their way among the injured, offering them solemn gratitude. By the time they were done, the only light came from mage-torches.

Meda called for their mounts, then said to Dally, "Ride with me."

They crossed empty fields, their way illuminated by Myron and Edlyn and the rising moon. Dally was exhausted now, more tired than she had ever been in her entire life. Holding to the reins and staying in the saddle required enormous effort.

Meda moved her horse to walk alongside Dally and surveyed the night-clad surroundings. "None of the valley's occupants came out to witness this battle. I find that most curious indeed. Can you explain this to me, Dally?"

"These days, most pretend the valley is content to be cut off. It gives them hope despite the unseen dangers pressing in on all sides." Dally willed her mind to wake from its half-slumber. "But their world is growing smaller with each passing season. All the routes joining us to the outside world run through the forest. Or rather, they did."

Meda pointed back to their right, where the eastern hills cut a distant silhouette from the stars. "What about through the mountains?"

"The trails have not been used in generations," Dally replied. She knew because the valley elders had often discussed this very topic at Norvin's table. "It's two days' ride from Honor to Eagle's Claw, the Ashanta settlement. You'd need permission to cross their territory. And it's said that the hills hold no water. Beasts wouldn't survive. Plus our main markets are in the other direction."

"So the locals . . ."

Dally found talking helped keep her weariness at bay. "Life was so good here for so long. Many locals always resented the outside world. We're not on any trade route. The nearest market town is four days' ride. Or rather, it was."

Edlyn said, "Surely they've noticed the thorn wall tightening its grip."

"The farms closest to the forest complain bitterly," Dally said. "I heard some of my former neighbors call it the silent invasion. But there's so much land around here. Between Honor and the Ashanta village there's not a single settlement."

"We were talking," Meda reminded them, "of why the locals did not offer us their support."

"Many elders claim we're better off without the outside world," Dally replied. "Especially after reports started coming in about the changes in Port Royal. And the new taxes. And laws that made no sense at all."

Alembord said, "You're very well informed."

"I served in the mayor's house. I listened."

"And you learned," Alembord said. "Can you read and write?"

"I attended the village school. Norvin insisted upon it."

Edlyn asked, "What did his wife have to say about that?"

Dally veered away from that. "The mayor owns many books. I've read them all. My favorites were those about the realm's history. And of distant lands."

Meda said, "Back to my question."

There was an easy pace to their conversation, one that left Dally feeling genuinely content. Even the languor of fatigue fit well. Her dogs were comforting shadows padding silently to all sides of their small group. She was among friends.

She said, "Most villagers want to imagine life is still under their control. Like it has been for generations beyond count. They claim the fiends simply don't exist."

They rode in silence for a time. It was only when Meda spoke again that Dally realized how angry the colonel had become. Meda asked, "Do the elders share this willful blindness?"

"Some. Perhaps most. They refuse to allow any discussion of what might be going on beyond the thorn wall."

"What utter nonsense," Alembord exclaimed.

"There are losses in the night," Dally went on. "Sheep mostly. A few prize steers. Three guards in four years. But they pretend it is bear or boar, for none have survived to say differently."

"Captain Alembord, as soon as we're back I want you to send out two fresh squads. They're to skin the beasts and return with their pelts." Meda's voice had lost all her former ease. "Order a troop to form cross ties from the halberds used in this battle. These spears are not to be cleaned."

"Aye, Colonel. Bloody they will remain."

"They're to salt the hides and then lash them to the halberds. And line both sides of the camp's entry."

"It will be done as you say, ma'am."

"The beasts exist," Meda said to the night. "The enemy is here and has been engaged. It's high time these locals see their world as it truly is."

13

Dally slept deeply and did not awaken until almost noon. She had been given quarters among the junior officers, which meant her berth was made private by way of cloth walls. The allotted space was scarcely large enough to hold her pallet, a chest, a collapsible writing table, and a stool. When she opened her eyes, Dally felt as though she had been transported to a ship of dreams. A gentle wind caused the walls to billow and shake. Sunlight turned the cloth translucent. Shadows danced with each passing figure. It was, in truth, as lovely a place as she had known in a very long while.

She discovered a pile of fresh clothes outside her portal. Dally followed the sound of splashing and entered the women's bathhouse. The water was drawn in straight from the river and was frigid enough to cause her to gasp. Just the same, it felt wonderful to be clean. She cut a portion from the hem of her former tunic, bound her wound, then dressed and went out to see her new world.

She entered a bustling village of cloth and wood. She followed the sound of dogs and found the kennel between the stables and the south river-wall. She greeted Bear, and together with the dog handler she inspected her two injured wolfhounds. Both seemed well enough. As she fed and groomed them, a trooper approached and said she was wanted in the officers' mess.

The vast cloth enclosure stood between the officers' quarters and Shona's assembly hall. Dally ate with a ravenous appetite and listened to the swirl of talk and planning. The side wall held a detailed map of the Three Valleys, which the officers used for setting out patrols and possible points for the next incursion. The talk was intent and specific. The battle was far from over. They had no idea how large a force they faced or where the next attack might take place. Nor did they understand why the enemy had taken aim at this region. Their planning was separated into two distinct segments—how to protect the villagers, and how to maintain the advantage in coming conflicts. Over and over Dally heard the same four words. Hold the high ground.

As soon as Dally was done eating, Myron gathered her up and led her to the training field. Mages formed a tight cluster by the outermost wall, an ancient dike so old the stones were almost lost beneath their blanket of moss and lichen. To Dally's left, young troopers practiced with pike and rapier, while the more seasoned soldiers hacked at each other with blunt broadswords. With this din punctuating his every word, Myron told her that Shona's wizards only had four wands among them. Shona's and Edlyn's and his own made seven. He and the Mistress were joining Shona's force for the duration, he explained. Dally found no need to ask how long that duration might be.

Myron then described the wands' making, the small gemstones created through ancient spellcraft from larger crystals called orbs that had been shattered in the battle for Emporis. Dally found herself marveling at the speed at which she was becoming a part of all this.

The energy and the earnest manner that Myron's students listened with was unlike anything she had known. The young mages were divided almost equally into nine boys and ten girls, aged anywhere from thirteen or fourteen to twenty. Myron was patient in the extreme, walking them repeatedly through basic spellcraft for harnessing their innate force, for shielding and attacking. They practiced with wooden sticks and sweated in the afternoon heat.

In truth, a great deal of these lessons were beyond her abilities. But Dally did not mind. In fact, she had the impression that Myron intentionally wanted the other acolytes to see her in this vulnerable and untrained state. So Dally exaggerated her lack of training and confessed repeatedly that the spells were beyond her ability.

When a soldier came to say Dally was wanted, Myron saw her off with a quiet, "Well done."

Meda met her in the open field before Shona's tent, surveyed her sweat-drenched uniform, and declared, "This won't do at all."

"Ma'am?"

"The elders are arriving. Shona wishes you to attend the audience. You'll need to bathe and change."

"Colonel, ma'am, I have no other clothes."

Meda frowned. "Wait here." She disappeared into the tent farthest from the officers' mess.

As Dally waited, she observed the last two halberds being fashioned into cross ties and the massive black pelt lashed tightly into place. The cross tie was then thrust upward and planted into holes dug alongside the passage leading into camp. There were thirty-seven of the pelts now, strung up like dark, doom-laden sails. There to transport the valleys into battle. Whether the villagers liked it or not.

Meda drew her back around with, "Here, lass. Go wash and change into this."

The outfit was so fine Dally was reluctant to even touch it. "Colonel . . ."

"Hurry, now. Shona wishes to speak with you before greeting the elders." Meda ended any further protest by turning away.

Dally washed hurriedly, then retreated to her little cubby. The new clothing was soft as a dawn breeze and shaded the gentlest of pastel greens. The colors swam and flowed under her touch. The outfit consisted of leggings and an under-tunic and a sleeveless outer robe. The robe drifted below her knees and was held in place with a jeweled belt.

When she emerged, Meda surveyed her quickly and demanded, "Where's your blade?"

Dally rushed back to her cubby and withdrew the rapier

from her chest. When she returned, Meda adjusted the scabbard and said, "Always wear your sword into audience with Lady Shona. It represents your willingness to bear arms in her name."

"This is hers, isn't it? The outfit."

"She chose it herself. I'm pleased to see I was correct, saying you two were of a size. Come now."

The audience hall was the largest tent of all and draped on both sides by tapestries that shone brilliant and alive in the afternoon light. A small wooden dais rose at the front and held a high-backed chair emblazoned with a gold crest. Two guards stood to either side of the empty throne. Four people gathered in the far corner—Edlyn and Myron and Alembord and the central figure.

Shona was lovely as the dawn. Dally had been granted no real idea of her physical appearance in their bodiless contacts, more simply an impression of the young woman's heart. Shona's dark hair ran like a bejeweled river down her back. She wore an outfit similar to Dally's, but colored royal purple. The robe's border was sewn with gold thread and tiny gemstones that glinted as she turned and gestured Dally forward.

Dally curtsied and held the position until Shona said, "Rise, my friend. Join us."

As Dally approached, she watched Shona return to her conversation. The young woman's countenance would have better suited a ruler three times her age. Shona was not just somber. She listened with a burning intensity. She spoke with a soft voice that carried the eminent force of command. Dally wondered if the young queen ever smiled.

Shona motioned for all but Edlyn to step away. She then said to Dally, "It is good to finally greet you in person, Dally. You are as fair as I envisioned."

"Thank you, my lady."

"Edlyn tells me you have the gift of far-seeing. I must ask, Dally, that you never seek me out unless there is an urgent need. A leader can never be seen to show too much favor." Shona must have detected Dally's disappointment, for she added, "I am doing you a service. Word will soon spread, if it has not already, of our secret bond. I'm surprised the village elders have not already come seeking to use this bond to their advantage."

Dally heard a tone of discreet bitterness in the words. "If they did, Norvin or his wife must have denied them access."

"His wife, yes. I have heard of this one. She is no longer your concern. But if others think you can provide access to power, they will show themselves soon enough."

Dally had the impression this woman carried the stain of great sorrow. And was as lonely as she herself had been. "My lady, might I offer you a gift of greeting?"

Edlyn said, "It is, in fact, a common courtesy when first meeting a royal."

Shona was clearly displeased with the title. But all she said was, "Very well."

Dally shut her eyes and reached out. In that instant, she knew which of her friends it must be. In fact, it seemed as though the bond was already being forged.

A few moments later, the runt of Dally's litter entered the tent. She trotted forward and halted by Dally's hand. "This is the smallest and the most sensitive of my friends."

"You're giving . . ." Shona's taut expression melted. "She's mine?"

Edlyn said, "You bought them all, my lady."

"That was merely to keep them as Dally's. The dogs are hers."

"And now this one is yours, if you'll have her." Dally motioned the dog forward. To her vast relief, she felt neither sorrow nor loss, only an immense rightness. She spoke the words she had often heard Norvin use. "Let her have a good sniff. Feed her a bit of meat. For the first few days, let her stay close. When you're ready, you name her. Short and sharp is best. My lady, may she serve you well."

14

Half an hour later, Shona seated herself upon the dais and told the guard to summon the elders. They entered the assembly hall in an uncertain cluster. There were several dozen altogether, perhaps as many as fifty, a third of them women. Some wore their finest garb, others looked like they had come straight from their fields. Which, of course, was their way of saying that they did not acknowledge this young woman as queen of anything.

And she certainly did look young. Shona's youth was accentuated by the two women who stood to either side of her high-backed throne. Edlyn was slightly stooped, and her face was creased by lines that Dally had not noticed before. Meda wore an unadorned uniform, a short sword attached to her belt and a well-used hilt of a war blade rising above her left shoulder. Shona herself wore the tunic of a battle mage. Her only adornment was the jeweled scabbard holding her wand

and the robe's crest sewn in gold thread. She watched the elders approach and waited.

Dally understood these Three Valleys leaders so very well. Many were not familiar, of course. But the set of their expressions told her all she needed to know. They had been somewhat cowed by their procession beneath the beasts they had spent years claiming did not exist. But they were also angry. Their little world had been shaken to its core. Their foolish claims and their haughty attitudes and their blindness had been both challenged and mocked. They could no longer lie to themselves and the other villagers that they were in control.

The greybeard who had complained over not hearing the tinker's news was a cantankerous sort who loathed change of any kind. He was, Dally knew, the worst possible choice as the elders' spokesman. But he had no doubt demanded that he be heard, whether they selected him or not. His beard jutted like an accusing finger as he said, "It's high time we know what's the meaning of your disturbing our peace with your coming!"

Meda's features drew back in a battle-hardened scowl, but Shona silenced the officer's retort with an upraised hand.

The elder took courage from the lack of response. His voice rose to the level he might use in scolding a grandchild. "Aye, and when are our farmers to be paid, that's what we want to know! A month we've supplied all your needs, without a by-your-leave for our troubles!"

Alembord shifted, standing alongside Dally by the left-hand wall. Shona glanced over, freezing him into position.

She did not address the guards captain because she did not need to.

"And what's to be the purpose of your coming?" The elder's stubby beard quivered in indignation. "We want safe trails to market, that's what we want. We want our borders pushed back to their proper station! We want—"

"What you *want*? You *dare* speak to me about your *wants*?"

The frigid fury in Shona's voice stunned them all, none more so than Dally. The queen rose slowly to her feet and stood glaring down at the elders. Her eyes blazed with a dark green fire.

It was then, in that frozen moment, Dally realized that for the very first time she thought of Shona as a queen.

"Do you think I *wanted* to be crowned at the onset of a battle for mankind's survival? This meeting has *nothing* to do with your wants!"

Dally watched the greybeard cringe away, like a cur fearing a blow. His beard quivered and jutted, but no sound emerged.

"We have come to your region *precisely* because the fiends have chosen this as their first point of attack. They too know you are isolated and unprotected. They sought to use this to their advantage. So we rushed here, intent upon rescuing you." Shona stabbed the air leading toward the exit. "Get out! The lot of you are dismissed!"

One of the women said, "But, Majesty—"

"Go! We will depart this region soon enough. And when the feral beasts of dread assault you next, when they drag away your children and set fire to your homes, you will *rue this day*!" When the elders remained clutching one another at the center of her audience hall, Shona snarled, "Alembord, you will escort this rabble from my sight."

"My lady." He motioned to the guards, who moved forward. "Outside and away, the lot of you."

But as they stumbled, shocked and terrified, toward the exit, one lone village elder turned back. "Your Majesty, I wish to offer my fealty."

"Hold, Alembord." The Lady Shona stood glaring down at the man who now stepped forward, separating himself from the others. "Your name?"

"Norvin, if it please my lady."

"Your village?"

"Honor, Majesty. I am its mayor."

Meda said, "You will address her as 'my lady.'"

"Honor," Shona said. "So you were my aide's guardian. Will your wife follow your lead?"

"My wife . . ." Norvin glanced at Dally. "She's had a hard go of it, my lady. She's not made for such times as these, and all the fears I've had to shoulder in my position."

"She had best learn to adapt, and swiftly," Shona replied, but without her former ire.

"Aye, my lady. She will." Norvin glanced at Dally a second time. "I promise you that."

Shona's gaze tracked with Norvin's. "What say you, Dally?"

"Norvin is a man of his word, my lady."

"And his wife? Colonel Meda and Mistress Edlyn did not think highly of her."

Dally remained silent.

Norvin broke in with, "My offer of fealty, my lady, it's for all the village. And we'll gladly give you these fields or any others for your use. If you'll stay. And protect us . . . from what's coming."

Shona studied him with a merciless intensity. Finally she said, "Go and speak with your clansmen. I will accept your offer of fealty, but on one condition."

"My lady?"

"It must be unanimous. Your entire village must attend me. Now go."

Dally ate that evening with the other acolytes. She only spoke when a young mage asked about village life. But that one question led to many others, about the elders and their spokesman and why the Lady Shona was so hard on the mayor's wife. Dally tried to be both frank and fair in her answers. But by the time she finished describing her former existence, she could see many of the acolytes now shared their leader's opinion. As she rose from the table, Myron nodded to her, an acknowledgment that she had succeeded in becoming one of their company.

As she prepared for bed, Dally recalled the Lady Shona in her audience hall, and the manner in which she had handled these self-important elders. She shut her eyes to the realization that in truth Shona's age held no meaning whatsoever. Here was a woman destined to rule. Mankind's survival, Dally decided, rested well upon Shona's slender shoulders.

That next dawn, Dally slipped once more from normal

slumber into that nether state. When a figure appeared before her, she first thought Shona had gone against her better judgment and come to visit once more. Then Dally realized this was a different person entirely.

The woman was surrounded by a most remarkable light. She seemed cloaked by a pale illumination, like a lantern seen through morning mist. Then she approached and spoke to Dally in an alien tongue.

Dally replied, "I don't understand you."

The woman was clearly shocked. "You are human?"

"I am."

"How can this be?"

Dally didn't know what to say, so she remained silent. She was surrounded by a fog that blocked her view of everything save this woman. They stood together on an unseen patch of solid earth, like an island suspended in the region beyond time.

The woman asked, "How do you come to walk the unseen realm?"

"I . . . have no idea. Until this moment, the only other time I did this was with Shona."

"And yet you are here. You are a mage?"

"Mistress Edlyn says I am gifted."

"So you are untrained. You serve the Lady Shona?"

"I do."

"Wait here."

As the woman turned away, Dally resisted the urge to ask where "here" was. The light that surrounded the woman dimmed slightly, but only for a moment. Then the woman said, “I am Bryna, the Seer in the settlement you know as Eagle’s Claw. You will pass on a message from my leaders to Lady Shona?”

“Of course.”

“Tell her that Joelle’s procession will pass her camp tomorrow at noon. Also the enemy prepares another attack. This one will come at the valley’s farthest boundary, on the village of Elmtree.”

Dally wasn’t sure how she found the courage to speak, but a question seemed to hover in the air between them. “You belong to our region. Which means sooner or later your people will be as threatened as us. Why will you not help fight this enemy?”

The words created a vibration that distorted Dally’s vision. She knew this to be a ripple of discord, a challenge to the harmony that bound this vision together. Even so, she was certain she had been right to speak.

The woman said, “One moment.” The pause was longer this time, but finally Bryna turned back and replied, “There is a disagreement among our leaders. To enter into this conflict breaks treaties that have been in place for over a thousand years.”

“As does having an enemy use magic to attack our region,” Dally replied. “Or Mistress Edlyn leaving the Long Hall. Or—”

Bryna stepped closer. “I agree. On all of this, I agree. But I have only just been appointed Seer, and there are many among us who, well . . .”

“Seek to remain secure within your borders,” Dally said,

and did not try to hide her bitterness. "Wish to stay blind to the threat these fiends truly represent."

Bryna took her time replying. "Your words carry a great force."

"The fiends burned down my home and killed my family."

"So you have as little patience with these elders as I." Once more Bryna turned away. When she returned, it was to say, "Tell the Lady Shona that I and my allies wish for you to accompany the procession."

Dally had no interest in going anywhere. She had not felt this secure or so bonded with others since losing her family. She said, "I serve the lady."

But Bryna was already gone.

15

To his credit, Norvin arrived early that morning along with every citizen of Honor. He was also accompanied by all the elders who had met Shona the previous day, including the greybeard who had addressed the regent with caustic disrespect. Four of the oldest villagers and three youngsters were down with a summer fever. Pallets had been fashioned, and the strongest among Honor's citizens took turns carrying them. At Shona's direction, an honor guard was formed up, both to greet the arrivals and to keep them from entering the camp proper. Instead, they were garrisoned in the meadow fronting the passage leading into Shona's hold.

Dally was counted among the guards, as were several others who had taken part in the battle. She could identify them from the way fatigue stained their features. She knew she probably looked the same way, but there was nothing she could do about that.

She had waited until well after sunrise to approach Shona's guard and ask for an audience. When she finished passing on her message, Shona and Meda both rebuked her for the delay. The next time she received a nighttime communication, Shona ordered, Dally was to immediately raise the alarm.

At a sign from Norvin, all the villagers knelt upon the earth, meek as little March lambs. They faced the guards and the camp, which meant they had a good long look at the double line of black pelts strung along the lane. The halberds' dark-stained blades glinted a silent warning in the sunlight.

As instructed, Dally was again dressed in Shona's finery. All the guards wore their dress uniforms. They waited there in the hot sun. Silent. The villagers grew increasingly nervous. A child fretted and was quickly silenced. From her position kneeling beside her husband, Krim met Dally's gaze and looked away.

Shona emerged from her tent, flanked by Meda and Alembord. Behind them marched an honor guard, and farther back came her small contingent of warrior mages led by Edlyn and Myron. For the first time Dally saw the lady's crown, a slender thread of intricately woven gold with a single gemstone positioned directly over her forehead.

Shona halted directly in front of Norvin. And waited.

Norvin fumbled his words. "Majesty . . . That is, Lady Shona, we wish to offer fealty."

Meda was the one who responded. She pitched her voice at a level just below a battlefield bark, intending to be heard by all. "Fealty in a time of conflict is a powerful oath. It binds both ruler and subject in a solemn pact. The Lady Shona vows to do her best to protect you and your region, even if it brings her and her army into harm's way. In return, you accept that her call to service, *in whatever form she deems necessary*, must be answered swiftly and without dissent." Meda gave a long pause, then demanded, "Is that understood?"

"Aye, ma'am, it is."

Alembord said, "You shall address her as Colonel."

Meda went on, "The oath of fealty is for life. There is no option for withdrawing. Disobedience or opposition will be treated as rebellion. Is that clear?"

"Aye, Colonel."

"And you still wish to make this offer?"

"Aye, we do."

Shona's voice was a soft counterpoint to Meda's verbal punches. "Do you speak for all gathered?"

"We are here with one mind, my lady. We answer with one voice."

"Well said, Master Norvin. You and your company may rise." And with that, Shona smiled. The warmth revealed in that silent gesture was enough to dispel all the previous day's ire. She bathed them with her pleasure. "Welcome to our ranks."

Norvin's face struggled to maintain composure, his relief was so intense. "Thank you, my lady."

Shona lifted her voice. "Good people of Three Valleys, I offer you two immediate gifts in return for your fealty. Dally, come here."

She stepped forward and curtsied. "My lady."

"Thanks to Dally's remarkable gifts, we have received

warning of a second attack by the dark fiends. What was the name of the village that is their target?"

"Elmtree, my lady."

Cries of alarm rose from one of the women and the greybeard.

"My stable master will equip those of you from this village with horses and a troop to see you home. Captain Alembord and the wizard Myron and four squads of advance troops will accompany you. Draw in all townspeople from your fields. Form barricades. I will shortly join you with the rest of my force."

The woman cried, "How much time do we have?"

"A few days at most. Not enough. Hurry." She raised her voice as they hastened away. "The rest of you are invited to remain. Water and sustenance will be brought. Our healers will see to those of you who ail. Colonel Meda."

"My lady."

"Present the mayor with payment."

Meda walked forward and handed Norvin a sack that clinked softly. Norvin opened it and gasped. "It's too much."

"You will dispense payment among all the villagers. The rest you will draw from in return for what you supply in the future. You will keep accounts and present them upon request."

Norvin fumbled in his attempt to reseal the pouch and bow at the same time. "My lady, it will be done as you say."

Shona addressed the gathering. "When the sun reaches its zenith, you must be prepared to kneel once more. Ashes of Hyam's slain wife will pass by, en route to her final resting place."

Trestle tables were laid out and a good fare was offered. Of course, almost all of it came from produce supplied by the villagers. But with Norvin walking among them and the lady's gold clinking at his belt, the gathering took on an air of muted good cheer.

Dally remained because she felt it was expected of her. She heard villagers speak of Hyam as a sturdy lad with good sense and a strong back. Others recalled his seasoned eye as a forest hunter. Many spoke of some mysterious field deep within the forest, passed down through generations, which few had ever seen. Then Alembord overheard their talk and regaled them with Hyam's life as a mage and emissary to the Ashanta. Disbelief turned to wonder as Alembord was joined by Meda, and the two of them described the battle of Emporis and the hunt across the yellow realm for the enemy who fought Hyam's company in the legendary city of Alyss.

Dally listened most intently of all, for she felt that hidden within these events were explanations for some of what befell her now. Her concentration was so intense, Norvin and Krim managed to approach her unseen.

Norvin greeted her with, "Many changes afoot. And it appears you're at the heart of them."

"I'm glad you saw fit to come," Dally replied.

"It was the only way," Norvin said, looking at his wife as he spoke. "Go on, my dear."

Krim's bulky form was taut and her throat constricted as she said, "I apologize for any slight or slur I might have offered you." She quailed as a grim-faced Meda stepped up beside Dally, one hand resting upon her sword hilt. Krim finished in a rush. "I hope there are no hard feelings between us."

Dally answered as she thought Shona would have wanted. "Thank you for your words." Her voice sounded flat to her own ears. "I accept your apology."

Dally turned away, wanting nothing more to do with that woman. Ever. She asked Meda, "Did you want me?"

"Lady Shona says to stand ready." The colonel turned to Norvin and said, "Prepare your folk, Mayor. It's time."

16

The troops directed the villagers in a roughish manner. Dally watched as resentment among the folk was erased by the realization that many of the soldiers struggled not to weep. The sight of so many battle-hardened warriors fighting against their own emotions was a harrowing sight. Not in the manner of causing fear, however. Instead, Dally wondered at what brought forth such affection from an entire army—soldiers who had been forced by events beyond their control to set all normal life aside, who had witnessed the loss of far too many of their company. And yet here they were, struggling to honor the arrival of a woman's ashes by not breaking down.

The soldiers directed the villagers to kneel facing the closest thorn boundary. As they sank down to the earth, Shona's procession arrived, led by Meda and Edlyn, all cloaked in black. They stepped forward and halted between the villagers and the thorn barrier.

The wind moaned slightly, as though groaning beneath its burden of grief. And then a portal opened.

Where before was an impenetrable fortress of branch and blade, now appeared a tunnel of emerald green. And from the portal stepped a second honor guard.

Of Elves.

The villagers gasped and murmured, then Meda turned and hissed. One sharp note. Enough to stifle all further sound.

The honor guard formed itself into two rows that flanked the portal. They moved in a slow, stately cadence, their every motion as precisely timed as heartbeats.

For Dally, everything changed. In the span of time between the green tunnel's appearance and the last Elven guard stepping into place, her entire perspective upon the day and herself went through a silent and devastating transformation.

While the villagers gaped in astonishment and the soldiers now finally saw fit to release their tears, Dally was released from time's hold.

In days to come, when she recalled the events, it seemed as though the spells binding the Elven kingdom reached forward to envelop her as well. There followed a series of impressions so powerful she jerked every time she recalled them. One potent bolt after another. They were not thoughts and they were not images. But they were both, and far more besides.

By the time the Elven king and queen appeared, the last image had already faded. And Dally knew what she had to do.

Behind the Elven rulers stepped a man robed in black, his face hidden by a cowl. He carried a black cushion, upon which rested a small urn carved from a single block of onyx.

Dally left her position by the villagers and stepped forward. As she did so, Shona bowed to the cowled man and then to the rulers and asked softly, "Hyam?"

The Elven rulers wore crowns identical to Shona's. They bowed in response, and the queen said, "He salutes my lady."

"I do not want his salute," Shona said, her voice breaking. "I want him here."

The king said, "My lady, even if Hyam had wanted to accompany us, our healers would have forbidden it."

"He is ill?"

"He is weak," the queen replied. "That is all they can say with any certainty. But something . . ."

"Something is wrong," the king said.

"He wishes you well," the queen said. "He has written you a letter which Connell carries, along with another from your parents, and one also from the Earl of Falmouth."

As Shona struggled for control, Dally knew she had no choice but to interrupt. From behind Meda and Mistress Edlyn, she curtsied and then touched the colonel on the arm. When Meda turned, Dally whispered, "I must speak to the rulers."

Meda's scowl would have blistered one of her troopers at thirty paces. She hissed, "It must wait."

"It cannot," Dally insisted. "This is vital."

Shona turned a tear-streaked face to the pair, but Dally doubted she saw much of anything. "What is it?"

"My lady." Meda saluted the Elven rulers. "This one claims to have a message."

Shona cleared her face with trembling fingers. "Majesties, this is Dally. She . . ."

Edlyn supplied, "She has the gift of far-seeing."

It was the Elven queen who said, "Approach us."

Thankfully, the Mistress of Three Valleys Long Hall stepped forward as well. At a sign from Edlyn, Dally curtsied a second time. "Forgive me, Majesties. But this cannot wait. The enemy will attack Elmtree at sunset tonight."

Dally's voice carried farther than she had intended, for Norvin called out, "The villagers will be destroyed! They have nothing save local guards to protect them, and Elmtree is three days' hard ride!"

The king studied Dally. "What sign can you offer that this warning is genuine?"

Dally was ready for that as well, though the act of addressing an Elven king caused her body as well as her voice to quaver. "Sire, you were intending to travel in procession to the Ashanta settlement at Eagle's Claw. You intended to join in their Assembly. But all this must wait."

"Must it."

"Aye, sir. The fiends are too many. They know their element of disguise has been lost. All their forces are gathering. They intend to sweep down the entire valley and destroy all the settlements."

It was Meda who demanded, "Do you know why Three Valleys was made their first target?"

"No, ma'am. Only that it is important to them. Vital."

Edlyn asked, "Is there a wizard counted among the foes?"

"All I see is a dark cloud, Mistress. A huge dark mass at the center of the fiends."

The queen said, "Dally, your name is a curiosity."

Edlyn said, "I suspect it is a shortened version of—"

"Dahlrin," the queen said. "Of course. It suits you."

Her husband said, "In this case, I suggest we all travel the green road to Eagle's Claw together, lay the Lady Joelle to rest, then return here to gather your forces—"

"Forgive me, sire. But there is more." Dally turned and signaled to her wolfhounds, who were now clustered by the camp's entrance.

"What magnificent beasts!" the queen exclaimed.

Dally pointed to the lead female. "Majesties, this one here is named Dama. I wish to make this a gift to Hyam."

The king brightened and said, "This could be a very good thing indeed."

Edlyn added, "This second one here apparently wishes to be known as Nabu."

The Elven ruler frowned, but before he could speak, his wife said, "As it should be."

The king was clearly taken aback. "Are you certain?"

"The past is now, my husband," she replied. "The naming is but a sign."

Dally bowed and motioned the other dogs forward. She said to Edlyn, "This female is yours, Mistress. Colonel Meda, please accept the male. And his brother is for Alembord. Majesties, yours is the one on the right. And the one there is meant for Bayard, the ruler of Falmouth Port."

In the silence that followed, a bird sang a note that to Dally sounded as piercing as crystal chimes. She found herself weeping, though she needed a moment to understand the reason why.

The queen said, "Most animals refuse to walk the green way, my child."

"Yours will. And the others, at least once, when I ask."

"This was shown to you as well?"

"Yes, Majesty. It was."

"In that case," the queen said, "I and my husband accept your gift with true and lasting gratitude. We consider it a new bond between you and this region and our own hidden realm."

Dally curtsied again and stepped back. She made no move to wipe away the tears. She knew they all thought it was over the loss of her friends. But parting ways with the wolfhounds had nothing whatsoever to do with this. They would remain bound to her regardless of where they went or whom they served.

Dally wept because the final image she had received when the Elven portal opened had held a message.

She was to leave the only home she had ever known. And she would never be coming back.

17

Dally walked the green lane and wished she could find it within herself to appreciate all she witnessed. She tried her best to look, to see, to remember. But nothing impacted her beyond the most superficial level. Her eyes took in the way the limbs wove together on both sides and high overhead, and how a living sort of light suffused every leaf and branch. She was aware that the passage of an entire army made no sound. She knew they walked for a time, and yet time did not touch them, for when they emerged from the tunnel and passed through the portal, the sun had not moved. Perhaps at some future point she would be able to recall all this and feel the wonder that escaped her now. But just then Dally was consumed by the tumult that overwhelmed her.

She stood at the back of the procession, blinking in the sunlight. Ahead of her, a line of white triangular stones marked the Ashanta boundary. A group of elders in white robes awaited them inside the perimeter. When Shona and the Elves passed inside the stones, Dally curtsied with the others. She joined in the long line that followed the silent Ashanta with their remarkable eyes of blue upon blue. They crossed over a pair of carved bridges and halted by a broad square stone. They interred Joelle's ashes where the stone met the emerald meadow, in sight of a city that gleamed white in the afternoon sun.

Shona spoke around her tears, then the Elven queen, and finally a young Ashanta woman. Dally recognized the voice from her dream contact as belonging to Bryna. Dally knew she would soon need to step forward and introduce herself. But all the while her mind was filled with questions for which she had no answers. They rose and fell in crashing, silent waves that rocked her at the level of heart and sinew.

Dally's questions held the same force as the images that had assaulted her when the tunnel opened beside Shona's camp. They were as insistent as battle spells, thrusting themselves deeply into her being. Only this time she had no reason to turn to others, beg for their help, tell her how to make them go away.

Who was she really? What did she seek to do with her life? Her past had been stripped away, the prison of her former existence gone. She was free, and yet Dally did not know what the word even meant. What course did she wish to chart for herself? She found herself struggling not to weep, though many of those gathered here bore tear-streaked faces. She was wracked by a sorrow that made no sense. She had a purpose. She had gifts. Her life held meaning. Should she not be thrilled? Where was the joy?

In the silent, sunlit warmth, Dally realized she had no idea what she wanted. The confusion was as powerful as guilt, though she had done nothing wrong. She felt herself being reshaped by the questions, as though images that had not yet appeared required her to ask what she had spent years fleeing.

Worst of all was the simple fact that she did not even know her own name.

With a start Dally realized the service was over and Bryna had sidled up to her unnoticed. The woman spoke slowly, and with an accent Dally had not detected in their previous meeting. "You have seen beyond yourself once more."

Bryna's manner of speech pushed aside Dally's confusion. "How do you know?"

"I can see it in your eyes. You struggle on your return, yes?" Bryna must have found what answer she sought in Dally's silence. "The way your being is wrenched does not ever completely depart. I use the correct word, yes? Wrenched. You feel . . ."

"Like I don't know who I am. Yes."

"Joelle taught me the human tongue. I have not used it since she was poisoned. Forgive me if I do not speak correctly."

"You speak it fine."

"I am this settlement's new Seer. For just a few weeks. The old woman perished before I was ready. But I have no choice now. These are dark times, and my role is vital to our survival."

The woman's eyes were her most remarkable feature. There was no white to them at all. The blue was so deep it appeared almost black. Dally decided it suited her features, which were as placid as living wax. "How did you know to come to me?"

"Ah. Yes. That is the question, is it not? I am not sure of the answer. I doubt my old teacher would have known the answer. She was one of those . . ." Bryna went silent at the Elven queen's approach.

The ruler of the green kingdom said, "Please continue."

Bryna showed surprise. "You speak the common tongue?"

"The old barriers are falling. We must adapt."

"I wish my leaders agreed with you." Bryna watched as the Ashanta leaders bowed to Shona, then again to the small grave, and started back. "My late teacher tainted every report with her distaste for the world beyond our boundary stones."

"She told your elders what they wanted to hear," the queen replied.

"What some want, perhaps most. The argument flows back and forth. And because no decision is reached nor action taken, those who seek isolation count each day as a victory."

"They are wrong." The queen radiated angry disapproval, but her voice held to its mild tone. "They failed my race once before with their dithering. May it never happen again."

Bryna nodded. "So say I and many others."

"We must depart. Dally has informed us that the enemy plans another attack this very day."

"I am expressly forbidden to join you." Bryna's voice showed a sorrowful yearning, soft as a sigh of forest wind. "Some are furious that I have made a far-reaching contact with a human."

The queen repeated more softly, "They are wrong."

"I and my allies agree with you." Bryna reached under her robe and withdrew a wand. "We offer this as a sign that we shall join you as soon as we are permitted."

The queen's gaze tightened as she inspected the letters carved along the staff. "That writing . . ."

"Milantian. I found it in our deepest cellar. There is no record of its presence. No one knew it even existed until it called to me."

"When did this happen?"

"Immediately after I was drawn to meet with Dally."

"Then it is hers." To Dally the queen said, "Take it."

"But . . . the Milantians . . ."

"Are the enemy," she confirmed. "And yet the stones of power know no allegiance. Good or evil, that is the mage's decision."

She accepted the wand with numb fingers. "Thank you, Bryna."

"I add my gratitude to hers, Bryna. May you and your allies succeed. We need your help." The queen touched Dally's shoulder. "We must be away. The enemy is coming."

18

As Dally approached the Elven portal, she was struck by another onslaught of images. She felt a sudden flash of revulsion over her loss of control. So much of her life had been spent enduring the helplessness of being young and alone. The very idea that she would enter into this new life and yet be forced to endure more of the same made her very angry indeed.

She tried to push the images aside. Refuse to accept them. But it only seemed to make the experience more powerful. As though they would use whatever force necessary to imbed themselves into her heart and mind.

Then it was over, and Dally found herself bent over with her hands on her knees, gasping for breath. Dreading the whirlwind of confusion and emotions that she feared would now beset her.

Edlyn stepped close and demanded, "What is it?"

Dally forced herself to straighten, then swayed with dizziness and would have fallen. But the Long Hall Mistress took hold of one arm, and the Elven queen the other. She saw the concern in their gazes, one smoky grey and the other crystal green. She saw the need and the urgency. She saw . . .

Dally said to the Elven queen, "Your name is Ainya. The name of the ruler's consort is supposed to be secret, held in trust by the citizens of your realm. You offered it to Hyam and to Joelle as a gift of trust and alliance."

The queen's hand dropped away.

"I don't know why I was told, but I was."

Edlyn offered, "It is a sign that the rest of what you have to say is true."

The anger still surged, granting Dally the courage to say, "That doesn't make any sense. You've believed everything else I've said before now."

But Edlyn simply stepped closer and said, "What's the matter, lass?"

"I don't . . ." She shook her head. That would have to wait. "You need a bond to the earth's energy to recharge your wands. There's a small one under Shona's camp. But a much stronger river of power runs beneath these headlands." Dally pointed to the rocky outcrop behind them. It flanked the forest and blocked the Ashanta settlement from being visible beyond the boundary stones. "You need to bring your wands here and prepare for the attack."

Up ahead, Shona must have realized the last of their party had stopped. She returned and said, "You are making the army wait."

Dally turned to the young ruler and demanded, "Why did you come to me that first time?"

Edlyn shifted over Dally's manner of address. But Shona lifted one hand to the Mistress and asked, "Is this a vital issue that must be raised now?"

"I'm not . . . Perhaps."

"The answer is, I don't know. I have never done anything like that, before or since." Shona unclasped her black robe and took it off. As she spoke, she folded it and held it in front of her. "My council and Oberon's had been debating where to make our first foray into the realm. Then Elven scouts brought word of the enemy's buildup around Three Valleys. We were already coming here to intern Joelle. It seemed a logical step. And we hoped that Hyam . . ."

"He will not be coming." Dally disliked the harsh, grating tone she heard in her own voice. Hated even more the pain it caused Shona. But there was nothing she could do about it. "Hyam is not exhausted. He is afflicted."

"Just as I suspected," Edlyn said.

Shona demanded, "What ails him?"

"I was not shown." Dally pointed back to the Ashanta settlement. "I only know that I am to return here. And beg them for their help. Either they give it, or . . ." She did not finish. She could not.

Ainya asked, "Is there anything else?"

Dally tried to shove the terrible image of the coming battle aside. She said to the Elven queen, "You have a special means of granting outsiders access to your realm. A crystal pipe or tube or something."

Edlyn and Shona gasped together. But Ainya merely nodded and said, "You will have it."

Dally knew she should thank the queen. But just then the internal tumult rose once more. The image of her returning and asking the Ashanta for help had carried two end results. If they agreed, there was a chance the battle might be won. Not a certainty, but at least there was reason for hope.

The second outcome had Dally pressing her fists to her middle and struggling to remain upright. Smoke and cinders enveloped her, as all the world she had ever known was reduced to death and ashes.

19

The rest of the somber company departed. But Edlyn stayed with Dally there by the Elven portal. The Elven queen remained as well, along with one elderly attendant. The sun was hot and the day silent, as though the Ashanta's preference for quiet reached beyond the distant boundary stones and dominated this borderland.

Dally could not hide her fear over everything the emerald tunnel represented—the surging power of further images, the tornado of confusion to follow, and most of all the loss of control. Not even her mind or heart were hers then. Not even the secret recesses where she had dwelled and yearned and hidden away all the sorrow of being left alone in the world . . .

Edlyn's voice broke in. "My dear, there is little in your recent history that gives you reason to trust anyone. Much less strangers like us. But I ask that you do just that." She gave Dally a chance to respond, then went on, "There is clearly something else to your message that troubles you deeply. Something—"

"It's not the message," Dally said.

Edlyn folded her hands inside her robes. Her back was impossibly straight, her eyes clear as the sky overhead. "Will you explain that, please?"

Dally struggled over the words. She hated talking about herself like this. Especially to people as powerful and potent as these two women. But their presence indicated an opportunity. And she needed help. Desperately.

The words came in fragments, and finally she stopped mid-sentence. The impossibility of it all stifled her ability to fashion another thought.

Edlyn said, "There are two issues that we must address."

"Three," Ainya said quietly. "Or four."

"Two that must be faced immediately."

"Either the Ashanta join with us," Ainya said, "or we face utter ruin at the hands of our dark foe."

Edlyn tsk-tsked. "We knew that already. Dally's final vision was merely a punctuation to our fears."

"Then what . . ."

"Dally has a gift," Edlyn said. "We must gain a clearer understanding. Else it could well take control and destroy her."

Dally reached up and gripped her throat, directly over where the gorge rose to choke off her air. The confusion had a name now, the fear a reason to coalesce.

In response, Edlyn reached over and took hold of Dally's free hand. "Calm, lass. We will solve this together."

"In case you've forgotten," Ainya exclaimed, "we are on

the verge of another battle. Which means time is not our friend."

Edlyn actually found that a reason to smile. "Forgive me, Majesty. But I have more experience with living in time's realm. We have hours yet. The army is being positioned. Your husband and his senior officer are discussing tactics with Meda and Shona. This could well be our only time to resolve these issues. And resolve them we must, else this young lady and her gifts might well be lost to us."

Ainya nodded. "Very well. Direct us."

"Dally, may I please see the wand Bryna gave you?"

Dally drew it from her belt and handed it over. The stick at its base was thick as her wrist. The gemstone at its peak was almost completely covered with petrified roots.

Edlyn studied it a moment, then passed it to Ainya and said, "Would it be possible to replace the Milantian's staff with one that represents our aims?"

At a gesture from Ainya, her elderly attendant took hold of the wand and spoke a soft word, and the ancient wood became dust in his hand. When the wand was destroyed, he held the clear glass up to the light and spoke.

Ainya said, "He detects no red force in the jewel."

"A thousand years in the Ashanta cellars," Edlyn said. "The taint has been cleansed."

When Ainya translated, the elder's only response was to draw the jewel closer to his eye. He spoke softly, causing Ainya to jerk upright.

Edlyn demanded, "What is it?"

"He is certain this is a heartstone." Ainya took the stone

from him and held it to the sun. The elder pointed and spoke, which Ainya translated as, "The jewel has all three signs. The oval shape. Its size is twice as large as most. And there at its heart, see the spark?"

"Remarkable indeed," Edlyn said.

Ainya handed the jewel back to the elder and spoke softly. He bowed in response and walked back toward the Elven tunnel. She told Edlyn, "I have asked him to craft for us a new wand in the ancient Elven tradition."

Edlyn watched the elder depart. "What does the heartstone signify?"

"So little is known about heartstones, and almost all of it is legend. Each orb has but one. Before today, only three were known to exist. Two form the center of the Elven crowns. The third is in Hyam's own wand. What they might do, what extra powers they might hold, we have no idea."

Dally said, "So that wand . . ."

"Belonged to a senior mage," Ainya replied. "That much is certain."

"Everything else must wait," Edlyn said. "My dear, here is what we know. Your gift of far-seeing is something normally known only to Ashanta."

"And Hyam," Ainya added.

"Hyam's bloodline is a mystery. You are the astonishment, Dally. You are human. Yet you possess an Ashanta power. What is more, your talent takes strongest control when you come in contact with the Elven realm. And an ally within the Ashanta has been called to offer you a treasure they did not even know they possessed."

The wind strengthened, causing the forest behind them to murmur its agreement. Far overhead, an eagle cried. Otherwise the valley was silent. Listening.

Ainya asked, "What does it mean?"

"Dally represents a hidden link," Edlyn replied, directing her words at the Elven queen. "We must assume that this is all intended as a message. What this might be, and what her presence represents in our current struggle, and why we have made this contact now, are the questions she must answer."

Dally jerked back. Not so much from Edlyn's words as from the spark that surged through her. A resonant force that shook her entire frame. "Why me?"

"That is part of the same question, one which you must commit yourself to understanding." Edlyn's gaze penetrated deep. "This defines your quest, my dear. We can offer you aid. We can help you develop your powers. But the quest is yours and yours alone. Refuse it at the peril of all mankind. Fail, and we shall no doubt perish with you."

20

The elder returned then. He was slender and scarcely reached to Dally's shoulder, which made the new wand look overlong in his small hands. He bowed as he handed it back to Ainya, who offered it to Dally as she might a royal gift. Ainya said, "My lady."

Dally disliked that title more each time she heard it. She did not know who she was, but a lady of the court most certainly did not figure into her character. But she merely took the wand and said softly, "It's beautiful."

The wood was so golden it glowed in the afternoon light. The gem was cradled within tiny strands carved like the staff, slender letters that flowed like the river down below where they stood.

Ainya said, "This is fashioned from the heart of our queen's tree. The tree was planted at the start of our reign and will form the pyre upon which I end my time in the

Elven realm. It is intended to signify the impermanence of all things."

Dally resisted the urge to weep. "You are very kind to me, Majesty."

"May it serve you well," Ainya replied. "And us."

"Come with me, Dally." Edlyn led her up to a broad, flat rock at the center of the headland. "This is where the image showed you that the power flowed?"

"Right beneath us," Dally confirmed.

"All right. I want you to try to follow my lead." Edlyn unfastened the cover to her pouch and withdrew her own wand. "This is a spell that not even all senior wizards can accomplish, so you mustn't worry if it's beyond you. Now take your wand in your right hand and close your eyes. Reach down with your senses. Beneath the rocks and earth where you stand is a river. You may not actually discern this. Very few can. It does not matter. What is important is that you forge a link within yourself, then bond with the heartstone. After that, try to draw the river up through yourself, into the stone. When you have done this, repeat this spell."

Even before Edlyn spoke the words, Dally felt herself filled with the sense of having already learned the words. As though the spell had formed a half-hidden portion of one of her impressions. The surging river of power was precisely where she had envisioned. The connection between herself and the force was immediate. Drawing it up was as natural as taking a breath, which she did. Through her feet, up her legs and her body, out her arm, down the length of the staff. When it touched the jewel at the wand's end, she shouted the words. It was not possible to simply speak them as Edlyn had instructed. The power did not permit her to be quiet or soft-spoken. She cried them with a force that shook the rocks beneath her feet, or so it felt to her.

Then it was over. Only this time, Dally felt no crushing sense of confusion or mental disorder. Instead, the bond with her wand was such that the power seemed to reflect back into her being. Her bones vibrated, almost like they sang a song she had yearned to hear since childhood.

She opened her eyes to find that Edlyn and Ainya and the elder had been joined by Myron and Shona's mages and a contingent of Elves. And all of them, each and every one, gaped at her.

Dally understood why, but not how. The gemstone at the wand's tip burned with a light that flowed from one color to the next, green then gold then blue then clearest white. And with each shift, Dally's vision underwent a change as well, for the light surrounded her. It seemed as though she saw the world through constantly shifting veils.

Myron asked, "Have you ever seen anything such as this?"

"Not once, not ever," Edlyn replied. "Majesty?"

Ainya shook her head. "What do you suppose it means?"

21

By the time Edlyn had instructed those mages who were up to the task of charging wands, the sun almost rested upon the western tree line. Shona arrived and charged her own wand. She spent a few moments in conversation with her senior mage and the Elven queen. All the while, her gaze drifted toward Dally, then away. Dally had no idea how to react, but as the young queen did not motion for her to join them, she remained apart. Shona started to walk her way, then seemed to change her mind and retreated to the Elven tunnel, accompanied by Alembord. Dally watched her departure and wondered if perhaps she had done something wrong.

Soon after, Edlyn led the remaining company back toward the forest boundary, where Elven guards waited with their queen. There was no portal to be seen from that distance, of course. But Dally knew it was there. She could taste the portal's magic like a spice in the air. The magic drew her forward and repelled her at the same time. She started to ask Edlyn if all mages could detect such a presence, when she was struck by another image.

This one came and went in a blistering assault, a blow to her senses and mind both. One quick flash was enough for her to stumble and almost fall. But the nearest mage caught her and kept her upright. Dally mumbled her thanks and tried to manage under her own steam, but as Ainya hastened them along the emerald tunnel, the only thing Dally saw clearly was an image that was no longer there.

When they arrived at the tunnel's far end, Ainya spoke to the Elven warriors in a tongue Dally loved without understanding what was said.

Ainya then told Edlyn and her contingent, "I asked if everything was prepared. My captain replies that all we need is an enemy. For they have seen nothing."

"The fiends are there," Edlyn said. "Of that I have no doubt whatsoever. The lass has been right on every score thus far."

When Ainya translated, the Elven officer frowned but said nothing more.

Dally started to speak, but her natural shyness blocked the words.

Edlyn's tone became sharp. "Young lady, you are forbidden from such hesitations, do you hear me? Forbidden! Lives depend upon your words."

Dally nodded and said to Ainya, "I reached out when I was in the forest. Before the first attack."

Ainya spaced the words well apart. "You . . . reached . . . out."

Edlyn said impatiently, "As she does with her dogs. Go on, Dally."

"They have the capacity to mask themselves. You see only shadows. But they are there."

Ainya had features carved from a rare stone, palest green, like a meadow seen through a dawn mist. Even her frown was majestic. "Can you reach now?"

"Do not ask that of her," Edlyn snapped. "If the enemy is there with his fiends, what then?"

"We need to know," Ainya insisted.

"We *already* know," Edlyn said. She motioned to Dally and the others. "Come. The army awaits us."

22

As they exited the portal, Dally was once again captured by the moment's sheer *potential*.

She slowed and allowed most of the company to move ahead. Before her rose a village she had never seen before, but one she knew from conversations and books. Three Valleys was a misshapen fork laid out from east to west. The two northern tines had streams, the southwestern finger held the river. Cliffs rose in the distance, tightening around the river and forcing it through rapids. Dally heard the rush of water, a constant murmur that never ceased, not even in the dry season.

But there was no time for that.

Dally reached out a hand without actually seeing whose arm she gripped. She could only say it was a man. She had not really seen any of the wizards and acolytes who had joined them on the escarpment. Now she regretted the lapse.

She whispered, "Say nothing and guide me."

An unfamiliar voice murmured, "As you say, my lady."

"Slow down," she said.

Even after he did so, she stumbled and might have fallen had his free hand not gripped her other arm. "I have you, my lady."

She had only a moment to notice how he did not ask if she was all right, or inquire after this or that. Instead, his hand and strength and sheer presence offered a sense of something more powerful than just supporting her body. He was there for her. Without questioning. Which was very good indeed. For she was about to do what Edlyn would no doubt have forbidden.

Instead of being impacted by another invasion of images, Dally allowed her awareness to extend. Though perhaps "allow" was not the proper term. She had no idea whether she could have fought against the moment's sheer intent. The one thing she was absolutely sure of was, this needed doing.

The forest was a dark hulking presence behind them. There was no hint of peace or calm to the woodlands, as she had known throughout her childhood. Of course there had been dangers then as well. But the threats had been well defined. So long as they were careful, she and her brothers had been free to skip along its boundary, gathering berries and filling hours with their pretend adventures. All that was gone now. Lost to the shadows that hid the beasts.

They were there. So many she could not count them, a great heaving mass awaiting the signal to strike.

In the space of half a breath, Dally saw that the beasts were controlled by a different sort of enemy . . .

And then the enemy realized she was out there. Exposed. Vulnerable.

The fury that swerved toward her was terrifying, like she had slipped over the edge of a volcano and was blistered by the rising heat.

Dally withdrew as swift as her cry for life. She clutched at the man. "Help me!"

Edlyn rushed back. "What is it?"

"There is something back there," she said, shredding the words. "A force or beast of a different kind. Something. In control."

"And the fiends?"

"So many." Shudders wracked her frame. "Hundreds."

It was only when Dally heard Shona's voice that she realized the young queen had joined them. "Go back and warn Ainya."

"At once, my lady." Then the man's hands were gone. The loss of his strength caused Dally to whimper.

"I have you, child. Myron, rush ahead and alert the others. The rest of you, to your positions. Hurry!"

Dally tried to clear her vision and find the man who had held her upright. She felt bonded to him in a manner she could not describe, not even to herself. But she merely caught a glimpse of his back as he raced away. She wanted to turn around and follow him. Speak words she could not bring herself to form.

23

They gathered on the tallest roof in Elmtree. Two rows of dwellings separated them from the western fields. Beyond the verdant summer countryside rose the forest. Farther away, distant cliffs formed a darkening silhouette. The last lingering traces of sunset painted an umber wash across the western sky.

Their rooftop belonged to the village hall. To their right, a stone watchtower pointed at the first evening stars. The roof's opposite end extended into a broad balcony, from which wandering minstrels performed in happier times. This Dally learned from the greybeard elder, who spoke of his village in fractured sentences. He and a female elder and Alembord and their escort had been found upon the road by Elven scouts, who had ordered them to abandon their mounts, as most animals refused to enter the forbidden realm. Then the company was returned to Elmtree by way of an emerald lane. The experience of traveling along the magical road had rendered the female elder mute and turned the greybeard into a man who sought to apologize without actually speaking the words.

All the villagers were barricaded in their homes, save those who were handy with a hunter's bow or blade. The outlying homes and hamlets were emptied. Those refugees were safely housed farther back in the village.

Dally was very glad indeed not to have a major role. She held back from the leaders clustered by the rear railing and wished she knew a healing spell. One that would knit her mind and heart back together again. Or, failing that, one that could offer some temporary comfort. She felt as though a vital piece of herself had been torn away by her bodiless search. Several of them, in fact—one for each time she had moved beyond the reach of her physical senses.

Dally feared this internal cavity would only grow larger. Each impact of these far-reaching images cost her another essential component of her being.

She tried to tell herself that it was merely a passing sorrow. She would heal, she would move on, she would serve a vital purpose. She had a place. And a future. She tried to make these words real in her mind through repetition. Just as she had done in her darkest hours, fashioning her little light against the surrounding night and cold and damp. And yet this fear gnawed at her. Just as it had when she cowered inside the mayor's shed.

Was this to be her destiny? To use a gift of such immense potential only to have it nibble at the very core of her being? Had she escaped one misery only to sink into another?

As dusk faded, Dally saw herself as she would be years from now. A crabby old woman bent over a cane, her back as twisted as her scowl. She screeched at everyone, dogs and birds included. The children laughed and threw stones at her. No one even bothered to know her name. Mad, babbling about voices and events that mattered to no one but her. Alone.

Dally turned from the group of leaders and did her best to push away the unwelcome thoughts. But in their place rose an even bleaker image.

She recalled the moment she had sensed the enemy.

Dally knew with utter certainty that she had barely escaped with her life. Just recalling the instant when the enemy had turned her way filled Dally with a sense of inevitability. Sooner or later, she feared, the enemy would find her. Then he would consume her mind and heart and . . .

Turn her into a slave. Only half alive. Never to be free again.

She did not think this. She *knew*. That brief glimpse of the enemy's fury and lust for destruction still blistered her.

Then Nabu and the one other remaining wolfhound pressed their noses into her thighs.

At first Dally thought it was because they sensed her distress. Then she realized that was not the case at all.

These were wolfhounds with the white streak of warblood. They were bred for combat. They sensed what Dally had been unable to detect in her current state.

At that same moment, the dogs now belonging to Edlyn and Shona growled softly.

Dally said, "They're coming."

24

Edlyn's mages and Shona's own archers manned the roofs closest to the meadow, forming a magic-enforced semicircle. Behind them, the village militia and archers gathered behind secondary barricades. For a dozen breaths, there was no change. The dusk was almost gone now, the last lingering light fashioning a sea of murky images from the fields and forest.

Edlyn asked, "The Elves are ready?"

Ainya did not shift her gaze from the empty pastures. "For the third time, yes."

The strategy was Shona's, the planning Meda's, with some rather heated input from Darwain, Myron, Alembord, and various village elders who were determined to defend their village as they saw fit. But Shona silenced the arguments by issuing a calm series of orders, showing that her voice was the only one they all would heed.

Her plan was simple in the extreme. As most brilliant plans were, according to Edlyn.

Layer upon layer upon layer.

Force the enemy to fully commit. Reveal themselves and their tactics and their full power in the process. Shona and her forces would then be better prepared for the next assault.

The prospect that this was not the last battle, nor the worst, was what silenced the most rebellious of voices. This was merely preparation for what was yet to come. And to succeed, they had to support their ruler. They had to unite.

Shona's strategy was immediately proven to be not merely accurate, but vital.

As the last light of dusk shone dimly, three tunnels opened in the thorn wall. The shift would no doubt have gone completely unnoticed had the gathered forces not been so intently focused.

Three rows of vague lingering shadows separated themselves from the forest. It would have been far too easy to ignore them entirely, pretend they were nothing more than the spread of night's reach. These lumpish wraiths poured silently forth.

One of Shona's personal guards muttered, "Would you just look at that."

"Hush now," Edlyn said.

The invasion was impossibly silent, as though the shadows had no physical presence at all. Instead, the gloom reached farther and farther, aiming at the silent village.

Ainya whispered, "My lady . . ."

"Not yet," Shona replied. "Hold."

And hold they did. Shona's soldiers, dressed as village farmers, left the fields and trudged in mock weariness across the last remaining stretch of meadow. Drawing the enemy farther from the forest's safety.

Shona said, "Sound the first alert."

At a signal from a guard, the watchtower bell rang once.

These false villagers appeared to retreat in utter disarray. They shouted with alarm as they ran, calling questions back and forth, demanding to know what was the problem, why they were running, what was out there.

The lumpish shadows accelerated.

The soldiers poured through openings, then the barricades were sealed shut.

The fiends struck the barricades, and the defenders' fury was revealed.

25

Archers," Shona said. "Shields."

It seemed to Dally as though even before the bell struck twice, the sky was filled with a rain of arrows. They hummed through the air, softly whispering chords of death.

The fiends responded with bellows and flames.

Shona shouted, "Halberds to the fore!"

There were only a few wands among them, and those were kept hidden. But all the mages could manage shields. The troops armed with the long spears were protected from the belching fireballs as they reached across the barricades and stabbed hard.

And still the arrows flew.

In the chaos of battle, the town hall's roof remained a haven of quiet intent. Ainya said, "My lady, it appears the rearmost enemies are returning to the forest."

Shona said, "Mistress Edlyn, signal your team."

In response, Edlyn stepped well back from the railing and murmured briefly. A few seconds passed where nothing changed. Then Dally felt the air begin to coalesce around her.

A lightning bolt seared down from a perfectly clear sky.

Even though she had known what was about to happen, still the shock caused her to jump. They had discussed the tactic at length. How to alert Edlyn's most distant mages when the watchtower bell would be overwhelmed by the clamor of battle. And not, if at all possible, alert their foe to the leaders' position.

The flash came and went, but it was enough for them all to see the fiends massed upon the meadow. Hundreds of them. More.

They waited in silent tension.

Then two meager spells shot forth from positions to either side of their station. Silent blasts of force that rippled across the field, strong enough to cause the fiends in their path to tumble about. The masking shadows were blown away. But the spells did no real damage.

Nor were they meant to.

Two of Edlyn's mages and their supporting troops had all scratched themselves deep enough for the wounds to bleed freely. And then the same spell as Dally had used was cast forth. An insignificant display of magery. One that sprayed mists of fresh blood over the entire field, attempting to drive the enemy into an uncontrolled bloodlust and draw them to their doom.

The fiends bellowed with one insane voice and threw themselves at the village.

Shona screamed, "*Now!*"

26

Ainya stepped to the balcony railing. She lifted her hands and chanted words that sounded to Dally as melodious as death.

Edlyn murmured, "We hear words not spoken for a thousand years."

A crown appeared upon Ainya's head, with a stone of emerald fire at the center of her forehead. Her entire being glowed, brighter and brighter, until the village and meadow and thorns and forest and cliffs were all burnished by her light.

Then the stars turned green and began to fall from the sky.

At least, that was how it appeared to Dally. One after another descended to earth, a graceful display of silent power.

But wherever they touched the earth, the ground was blasted by green fire.

The fiends were taking terrible losses. And still the arrows fell.

From the forest came a low moan, a wordless howl that

went on and on. Those beasts still standing turned as one and raced back toward the forest.

Then the thorn wall burst into flames.

The light was blinding, an intense green inferno that rimmed the village on all sides. As far in every direction as Dally could see, the thorn barrier was ablaze.

And through the flames stepped the Elven army.

Shona called, "Archers cease firing!"

Both the arrows and Ainya's rain of destruction ended. The village's barricades were cast aside so that Shona's troops could attack, joining the Elves. Together the armies flung themselves at the beasts.

The assault turned into a rout.

Edlyn walked to Dally and said, "It is time, my dear. I want you to search without reaching out. I know that sounds impossible. But just the same, you mustn't make yourself . . ."

Even before Edlyn finished, Dally knew the answer. She ran to the railing and pointed at the darkest point in the forest. "There! He is there!"

Edlyn stepped up to her right, Ainya to her left. "Dally, raise your wand! On my mark, one, two, and fire!"

Dally only had the one spell. And she had never applied that with the wand in her hand. She had no idea what to expect.

The blast catapulted her backwards, but not before she saw a sheet of tightly focused fire stream out from her wand. Dally struck her head as she fell, and the last thing she saw was the final traces of her rainbow-colored fire streaming straight up—a fountain rush aimed at the stars. Then the night went blank.

27

Dally's first thought when she opened her eyes was, the man seated by her bed appeared to be everything she was not.

Self-assured, poised, handsome. And rich, by the look of things. He wore the warrior mage's grey uniform, only his was in the form of tailored trousers and overmantle and matching boots, with the Oberon insignia sewn into one side of his shirt and Shona's on the other.

He managed a regal bow even while seated. "A very good morning, Lady Dally."

She pried apart her dry lips and rasped, "Please don't call me that."

"Thirsty?"

"Very."

"Let me help you sit up."

When his hands settled upon her arm and the back of her neck, Dally realized it was the man who had aided her before the attack. She found it mildly remarkable how it was not his good looks nor his deep voice but rather his touch that she recognized. She felt once more an intense bonding. Which caused her to blush. She did her best to hide behind her cup.

"More?"

"Please."

"How shall I call you?"

"Dally is the only name I've ever known. Unless a childhood dream is real, and Dahlrin was indeed the name I was given at birth. As Mistress Edlyn suspects." She drained the cup. The water tasted exquisite. "Thank you for your gift of strength yesterday."

He offered another of his seated bows. "You are most welcome, Dally. I am Connell."

"You are a wizard?"

His smile was magnetic. "Some would dispute that claim, but yes. I am."

Dally looked around. Her pallet was surrounded on three sides by sunlit cloth. "I'm in the infirmary."

A grey-haired mage chose that moment to walk past. He saw Dally was awake, scowled at Connell, then asked her, "How are you feeling?"

She took stock and replied, "I'm not sure."

Connell asked, "Do you remember last night?"

The images were disjointed, all save the blast of multicolored power she had sent up into the stars. "Did I hurt someone?"

At a gesture from the medic, Connell rose and stepped away from her bed. "None of our company, if that's what you mean."

Cool fingers inspected the base of her skull. Only then did Dally feel the distant pain.

The healer asked, "Does that hurt?"

"A little."

"A little is good. A lot is bad. If the pain grows worse you must tell me."

Connell asked, "Can she go?"

Clearly the medic disliked Connell's presence. "There is no apparent damage. But head injuries surprise us from time to time." He said to Dally, "Remember, the first sign of rising discomfort, you must alert me or another medic."

When they were alone, Dally asked, "What did you do to upset the man?"

"Not me, but our leaders." Connell did not resume his seat. "If you are ready, there's something they desperately need for you to do."

Dally felt a shock of rising dread with the realization of why he was there. "Oh no."

"I'm afraid so." He offered his hand. "Will you come?"

The medic protested again as they departed the infirmary, but no one made a move to stop them. A low mist clung to the village of Elmtree, turning all edges soft and making it impossible for Dally to tell where sounds came from. Then a soft rush of footfalls was followed by a wet nose pressing into her side. Dally knelt in the damp earth and allowed Nabu to lick her face. The simple act helped immensely to anchor her to the moment.

When she lifted her head from the dog's fur, she saw the last remaining unnamed dog hovering just out of reach, waiting her turn. Dally reached out one arm. The dogs smelled of damp pelts and life. She gave in to the simple pleasure for a time, then rose and asked, "Why now?"

"They never tell me anything." Connell gestured toward the unseen camp. "Shall we?"

Beneath his glib words, Dally detected a faint bitterness. She knew the question was valid. Why did they want her to hunt for answers now? Somewhere in the distance she heard a pair of fiddlers practicing a jig and knew the village was preparing a fete. The battle was won. The legends had come alive before their very eyes. The thorn barrier was no more.

Dally walked alongside the tall mage and asked, "Couldn't their questions wait just one day?"

"Apparently not."

Gingerly she touched the point where she had struck the stone. "My head hurts."

Connell pointed into the mist. "Which is why an Elven healer is standing just beyond the portal. Or so they claim."

Dally said, "You know something."

"I suspect," he corrected. "I have watched powerful people not say things all my life. It has granted me a hard-earned ability to deduce what they keep unspoken."

His words almost made sense. "All your life you've been surrounded by power?"

"My earliest memories are of a prince's audience chamber. My family members are wealthy traders with a heritage stretching back to Falmouth Port's earliest days. They were the first to offer fealty after the Oberons retreated there. And they have reaped the whirlwind ever since."

All Dally heard made this man seem impossibly far removed. A universe of wealth and experience separated them. It was ridiculous to feel such disappointment. All she said was, "Oh."

"I learned early and well to hear what was not being said. And what they don't want to admit, not even to themselves."

"What did you not hear from our leaders today?"

He stopped and lowered his voice, though there was no one visible to overhear them. "Two things. First, they don't want to admit to something all leaders dread."

"What is that?"

"They have no idea what to do next," Connell replied. "Which leads us to the second unspoken message. They suspect the dark wizard who led the attack has survived. There is no evidence one way or the other. And the remaining fiends have vanished. The Elves have scoured the forest and found no sign. But they fear the true foe is still out there, and I agree."

Dally nodded reluctantly. "They need to know if he's going to attack again, and how."

"And where," Connell confirmed.

"They could ask the Ashanta."

"And they will, if they must. But the Ashanta are being extremely, well, Ashanta. So they'd rather ask you."

The mist coalesced into a dense white entity that threatened to cut off Dally's air. Even so, she managed a quiet, "I'll do it."

28

They passed by the kennels, where Bear greeted her warmly and directed her two wolfhounds into the makeshift corral. Then they left the village by the main road.

Dally leaned heavily on Connell's arm. The point where her skull met her spine throbbed. She felt no pain, yet she knew agony was there, bound into captivity but ready to burst out at any time. "How long will the medic's spell keep my pain at bay?"

"As long as it needs to. Just let me know if you feel discomfort. The medics reluctantly instructed me in how to strengthen it."

Her steps were unsteady and far too slow. But Connell matched her stride and showed no impatience. "Can't you just make it go away?"

"I am no medic. But I'm told that pain plays a role in the

healing process. Erase one, you stifle the other. Best to just keep it at a distance."

Dally found it very pleasant to rely on his strength. Connell exuded a refined masculinity, not so much a scent as a charge she could feel in the pit of her stomach. "Why are you here? I mean . . ."

"I know what you mean." He cast her a sideways glance, his eyes clear as washed sapphires. "How open would you like me to be, Dally?"

She liked his directness and responded in kind. "Mistress Edlyn said she would always tell me the truth, even when it was far more difficult than a lie. I think that is the nicest thing anyone has said to me in a long while."

He nodded. "Very well. The answer is, we have something in common, you and I. The rulers we serve have no idea what to do with us."

"Me, I understand. But you?"

"Shona and I have a history."

Dally knew a flash of envy, which she quickly stifled. "Terrible word, history."

"I've known Shona since we were children. Our families thought of us as the perfect match. She is . . ."

"Beautiful," Dally said softly.

Connell's words slowed to match their pace. "Since her coronation, I've always expected to serve as her chief mage." He returned the salute of passing squaddies. "Terrible thing, expectations."

"What happened?"

"Shona selected Myron to lead her wizards. Sooner or

later Edlyn must return to the Long Hall. Oh, she's promised to return whenever Shona requires, and bring the hall's orb with her. But placing Myron in the lead position serves as a living bond to this vow."

"So they sent you to me."

"You need a teacher," Connell replied.

"I certainly do."

"I'm told I'm quite good at that."

"Do you mind?"

"Dally, I should be asking you that. Say the word, and Shona or Meda or Edlyn or Ainya will make me vanish."

Dally took her time responding. They left the trail and entered the meadow bordering the forest. She could not actually see where they were, but the ground was rougher here. The pasture was sown with summer hay and felt heavy with dew. Each step swished the damp softly against her legs. Then the first hint of what lay ahead came to her.

She said, "I would consider it an honor. And more besides."

Connell sketched a brief bow as they walked. "I am the one honored."

A few paces more, and she caught the first faint hint of the power that awaited her. "I'm so scared."

"Of what?"

But there was no way she could put her rising terror into words. The Elven portal was up ahead. And with it came another blast of everything wrong and unknowable about her life.

Connell stopped and turned to her. "What frightens you, Dally?"

"That." She pointed into the mist. "The force that is poised to swallow me again. Everything it represents. The risk that it will one day consume me entirely."

He studied her face with a worried gaze. When she did not say anything more, he asked, "Will you wait here, please?"

"Of course." Gladly. All day, if possible. Or a week. Longer.

Connell left her there in the knee-high grass and walked across the field. He was soon swallowed by the mist.

Dally found a comforting blandness to the fog. Sounds came from all directions and nowhere in particular. She felt surrounded by people intent upon protecting her. Dally relaxed in stages, gradually accepting that the pain in her head was truly kept at bay. She wished she could sit down. Better still, go back to the infirmary and lie on her pallet and pull up the covers . . .

"Dally?"

"Over here."

"Ah. Excellent." Connell reappeared, leading an older Elf whom Dally recognized as Ainya's aide. He spoke in that melodious cadence that Dally had loved ever since hearing the very first word. Connell translated, "This is Vaytan, and he asks if you would answer some questions."

"You speak Elven?"

"Some. I'm learning. Languages do not come easy to me. But Master Trace asked, so I study."

"Trace?"

"Another time, yes?"

The Elf spoke, then Connell said, "Vaytan wants you to walk forward slowly and tell him when the portal's force impacts you."

Dally remained where she was. "Now."

The two men halted in mid-stride. "Truly?"

"Oh, not like he means. I don't feel drawn away." She pointed slightly to their left. "But I know the portal is right up ahead."

The Elf's green-gold gaze radiated kindness and intelligence in equal measure. "He asks that you describe the sensation."

Dally thought Vaytan was probably quite old, though there was a sprightly brilliance to his manner. She wondered how Elves measured time, or if they bothered to even count the passing years. "It's like I smell it, but not with my nose. I'm sorry, I don't know how to say it any better."

"He says perhaps it's as if you have grown a new sense."

"Yes, that's it exactly."

"Can you smell all magic?"

"I don't have enough experience to know. But I don't think so."

Vaytan waved that aside and continued speaking.

"Good, he says. Very good. Now he asks you to walk toward the portal and tell him the instant you feel your sense of reality begin to shift."

The fears she had managed to set aside returned in a rush. "Will you hold my hand?"

"Dally . . . Of course."

The Elf noticed the exchange, and Connell translated, "Vaytan asks what about the act of far-seeing frightens you."

"He doesn't know?"

"He says there are ancient records of Elves with this ability.

But he has never met one. All Ashanta hold this gift in some capacity, or so he has been told. But the Seers are the ones trained to harness it. He asks again about your fears."

"I'm not scared by the seeing." Dally found a comforting strength in how the human mage and the Elven elder both treated her as, well . . .

She had to search for the word that described their attitude. An equal, she decided. Neither her upbringing nor her raw, untrained abilities mattered to them—at least, not enough for them to talk down to her. She realized this was the trait that had most appealed to her about all these recent experiences. Edlyn, Alembord, Meda, even Shona. They saw her as simply one of them.

Connell gently pressed, "If it is not the far-seeing, then what?"

"It's what comes after," Dally replied. "I'm attacked. Each time I far-see, another portion of my life is stripped away."

The two men exchanged worried glances. "Vaytan says, will you walk forward now, please."

Gradually her grip on Connell's hand tightened. Vaytan stepped closer. One step, two, three . . .

"Now," she gasped. "Here. It's started."

Vaytan's gaze was deep, penetrating, concerned.

"He says, we would not ask this of you if it were not so important."

"All right. Yes."

"Dally, would you loosen your grip a trifle?"

"Sorry."

"No, I'm the one who should apologize, pulling you from

your sickbed . . . Vaytan asks, what is the difference between what you sense now and looking into the candle?"

"In the candle, I travel somewhere, I see, and then I return. Here . . . I have flashes of insight."

"I don't know the Elven word for flash. Can you use another?"

She could feel the tendrils of power rippling through her gut, almost but not quite powerful enough to pull her away. "Lightning. Explosions. Bursts of force. Attacks."

"All right, all right." Connell's gaze mirrored Vaytan's concern. "He asks, might we ask you a question that directs what you will receive as images here, as the Mistress did with the candle?"

"I don't know. Perhaps."

"Can you explain?"

"I tried to direct it once already." Her responses were brief gasps of words, all she could manage. "I knew Edlyn needed to find the enemy. So I looked. And there he was."

"Vaytan says this is very important. We do not seek to have you see something that is out there. We already know about the issue as it appears. Do you understand what he means?"

Dally found it too difficult to speak now. She nodded, or tried to. But perhaps it was merely a shudder.

"We do not need you to go and see something," Connell repeated. "We need an answer to an unresolved mystery. If there is indeed an answer to be had."

Dally heard the dialogue on both sides. Musical chanting, then Connell. Two lovely voices, so close she felt their warmth. And concern. She nodded again. She was terrified. But she was also ready.

"We need to know what is wrong with Hyam. And how we can heal him." Connell gave that a moment, then gripped her arm with his free hand. "We are with you, Dally. Step forward when you're ready."

29

Once again, Dally woke to sunlit cloth walls and an elegantly handsome man seated beside her sickbed.

As soon as she opened her eyes, Connell rushed from the room. He was gone long enough for Dally to realize that the sun now shone upon the western wall and carried the burnished warmth of approaching dusk. Which meant she had been unconscious through the entire day. Dally's worst physical discomfort came from a very sore throat and the throbbing juncture where her head met her neck. But she also felt internally bruised, as though her deepest being had been assaulted by the morning's events.

Which, she decided, was more or less the truth.

She heard approaching voices and pushed herself to a seated position. Her dizziness was so intense she felt nauseous. But she was desperately thirsty and did not want to try to drink lying down. She required both hands to lift the mug on her bedside table. Each swallow was agony, but the water tasted divine.

The voices grew into a fierce argument swiftly approaching. Dally wanted to be standing for whatever was about to come her way, but her legs would not support her.

The healer protested, "I allowed one of your parasites in there because the Lady Shona ordered. And that is one too many!"

Connell said, "Parasite? That's a bit harsh."

Meda snapped, "Healer, you forget yourself."

"I forget *nothing*!"

"What is more, you forget whom you address!"

"I know *exactly* whom I'm addressing! What's more, I know *where*! In *my clinic*!"

Edlyn said, "That's quite enough."

"You took one of my patients before I gave my permission. You placed her in harm's way. You brought her back in an even worse state. And now you want more of her! No, I say! No!"

Meda snarled, "Alembord, restrain this medic. And if he gives you any further trouble, cage him."

Shona's was the only voice that remained calm. "You will do no such thing. Connell, where is the patient?"

"The last compartment on your right, my lady."

Even as wounded and dull as she felt, Dally knew a keen nervousness as the group forced their way past the medic and crowded into her doorway.

The medic kept struggling against Alembord's firm hold. "I order you to *release* me!"

"All of you be silent." Shona approached the foot of the bed, her voice and face holding a deceptive calm. Dally thought her force was made even more potent through this evident control. Dally struggled to rise, but Shona ordered, "Stay where you are."

"My lady."

"How do you feel?"

"Not good. But it doesn't matter."

"Of course it matters," the medic groused. "Do you not hear her? The woman is ill and needs—"

Shona merely turned and glanced his way. A single look.

The doctor froze like he was made of glacial ice.

Shona said softly, "I want you to assure me that you are quite done."

The medic made do with a single nod.

"Alembord, you may release the healer. Meda, take your hand off your blade. Edlyn, sheath your wand." She turned back to Dally. "How much do you remember?"

"I'm not sure." She swallowed painfully. "My throat is very sore."

"I'm hardly surprised. After the way you shouted."

"I . . . yelled?"

"Screamed, more like," Connell said. "On and on."

Edlyn stepped forward, took the empty cup from Dally's hands, and gave it to the medic. "Make yourself useful, good sir. Tepid this time, and lace it with honey and lemon."

Dally asked, "What did I say?"

Shona's resolve almost broke. "Hyam. You repeated his name. Many times."

Dally remembered then. The name had been at the heart of a surging blast of images. She said hoarsely, "Hyam is dying."

The queen struggled momentarily but maintained her composure. The only evidence Shona gave of her internal destruction was the release of a single tear.

"My lady . . ." Dally watched the tear's descent.

"Honesty," Edlyn said softly. "Remember its value. Even when it hurts."

Dally found it necessary to focus on the Mistress to continue. "Hyam is wasting away."

"Poison?"

"Not in the normal sense. Nothing he has taken. But it is the enemy's hand at work. The image was clear on that."

"Just as I suspected," Edlyn said.

"But how?" Shona's voice was as soft as it was woeful. "He has remained shielded inside the Elven realm since Joelle's death."

"Perhaps from before," Meda said. "In his quest for the vial."

The healer took the mug from an assistant and passed it to Dally. He was now as caught up in the drama as the others. "Vial?"

"Joelle's life breath was forced from her body," Meda said, the former quarrel forgotten now. "A Milantian mage stole it away. And I watched it happen."

"You were as frozen and helpless as I," Shona replied.

"You were far from helpless, my lady. You saved my life."

She waved that aside and turned the name into a soft dirge. "Hyam. Is there anything we can do?"

"Probably not, my lady. That was altogether clear."

"Which means we should strike," Meda said.

Dally shook her head. "All the options you are considering, they lead to ruin."

Meda scowled. "How can you be certain?"

"Because I saw them." The recollections caused her entire body to shudder anew. "The proposed attack on Port Royal leads to utter defeat. Your plan to kidnap the king's wife and son is no more successful. A blockade of the Inland Sea would lead to complete—"

"Those plans are secret," the colonel hissed.

"No longer," Edlyn said. "If Dally has envisioned them, we must accept the risk that our enemy has managed to access them as well."

Shona said, "Go on, Dally."

"Every concept you have discussed would only lead to defeat and ruin. The enemy is ready. He hopes to use Hyam to lure us into a desperate act."

Shona demanded, "What, then?"

"My lady, there is little hope."

"A little is better than none at all!"

"I must go to Eagle's Claw," Dally said. "Alone, save for one guard."

"When?"

"Now. This very instant. There isn't a moment to lose. Hyam's life hangs in the balance. And ours."

Edlyn demanded, "What are you to do once you arrive?"

"The only thing I can," Dally replied, and sipped from her mug. "Wait."

30

At a word from his queen, Alembord departed to begin preparations. When Connell offered to serve as Dally's guard and liaison, the group seemed to have already accepted it as fact.

The medic fretted over Dally, but mostly in silence. Even so, Shona finally sent him away. When he departed, Shona said, "You repeated one other phrase."

"Over and over," Meda said.

Dally nodded. She remembered now. "The road. You must begin building it immediately. Connecting Three Valleys to Falmouth Port. The Earl of Oberon must start from his end. Today."

Meda protested, "This place is separated from Falmouth Port by a full month's trek."

"Nonetheless, the concept makes perfect sense," Edlyn

said. "If the enemy is indeed seeking to divide us and defeat us parcel by parcel."

Shona said, "In that case, a road from our Falmouth stronghold to this deep inside the realm would cut through the heart of his plans."

Meda shook her head through all this. "You don't know what you're saying. To forge a road directly between here and Falmouth means battling against mountains and wilderness and a dozen principalities allied to Port Royal."

"Allied to them now," Edlyn corrected. "Who knows where their allegiance would be if we were seen to offer a genuine defense."

Dally repeated, "The work must be started. Immediately."

Meda demanded, "But why?"

"I don't know."

"Enough," Shona said. "We have the message. We must discuss this with the Oberon council."

"And the Elves," Edlyn added. "We will need their permission. And their help, since it will cut through their forests."

Shona stared at the dimming light beyond the western wall and murmured, "I should be with Hyam."

"No, my lady," Dally replied. "You should not."

Edlyn asked, "Was that another of your impressions?"

"Stronger than that," Dally said. "Yes, it was."

When Shona continued to stare at what only she could see, Edlyn told the young queen, "This is no doubt the purpose behind the attacks on Hyam. Weaken our forces from the center."

Shona's only response was to wipe her face with trembling hands.

Edlyn reached out and draped an arm around the young queen's shoulders.

They stood there in silence until Connell returned and said, "We are ready to depart."

31

They left the infirmary just as the sun touched the treetops. Dally was carried upon a cushioned pallet by four troopers. She disliked intensely how Shona's company watched and worried as she passed. Edlyn and Meda accompanied her. Nabu and the unnamed wolfhound trotted to either side of her stretcher.

Dally wasn't sure how to react as work halted and most faces turned her way. She tried to tell herself that they cared for her, that she was one of them. But her past experiences with being the center of attention were harsh and painful. All she said was, "I saw myself doing this alone."

"You saw yourself alone at the Ashanta boundary stones," Edlyn corrected.

"Mistress . . ."

"That is what you said. Correct?"

Dally sighed.

"Fine. Alone you shall be. There."

"But—"

"Let's make this perfectly clear," Meda said. "You are not going to isolate yourself for however long this requires."

"The enemy is still out there," Edlyn said.

"The Ashanta must see me as alone and vulnerable," Dally protested. "That much was clear."

"And so you shall be." Connell pointed to where Alembord listened as Shona and the Elven queen discussed something with grave intent. "Alembord has erected the guards' tent by the forest. Your own is on the other side of the headland."

"No guards," Dally pleaded. "No soldiers, no blades—"

"I will be with you, but on my own," Connell replied. "Standing well back. Armed only with my wand."

Further protest was halted as they approached the portal. The Elven queen broke away from her discussion with Shona and walked over. "How are you?"

Dally struggled to rise. "Fine, Majesty."

"Stay where you are. And treat me as an ally. I ask again, how are you?"

"I cannot find the energy to stand. Even my thoughts feel heavy. I feel as though despair is an enemy just waiting to attack." Dally gestured toward an invisible line, beyond which awaited the portal's force. "And I dread another encounter with whatever powers will assail me."

Shona said, "Our healers have done what they can. Which is to make her comfortable and little else."

Ainya reached up and allowed her fingertips to drift about the air next to her head. The crown appeared. "Show me your wand. No, keep hold of the hilt."

The Elven queen bent down and breathed upon the gemstone. It burst into a brilliant green fire. She began shaping the light so that it covered both Dally and her pallet. The entire world became viewed through a gemlike veil. Every living element, all the people and the animals and the smallest blade of grass, now carried the same emerald glow.

Ainya straightened. "The naming of a regent's spouse carries with it a series of responsibilities. One of them is the task of serving as the ruler's last line of defense. I want to see if this might shield you from yet another experience as we travel."

Dally didn't know what to say except, "Thank you, Majesty."

Ainya remained where she was, gazing down at Dally, the jewel at the center of her crown burning with a fierce light. "You will carry a message from me to the Ashanta?"

"Of course, Majesty."

"Tell them of the name you have bestowed upon your beautiful dog, and how this came to you. Then you shall pass on these words from me personally. Tell them that the past is now."

Dally found no shame in the tears that came unbidden to her eyes. "The past is now," she repeated.

"Tell the Ashanta that we shall endeavor to hold the field. Just as we did a thousand years ago. But we ask that they not show the same reluctance to join with us. The danger is too great. Together we shall vanquish the foes. Divided . . ."

Dally wiped her eyes and said once more, "The past is now."

"Now go." Ainya stepped back. "And may you succeed in your quest. For all our sakes."

32

Thankfully there was no hint of being assaulted yet again by the Elven force as they carried Dally along the emerald lane. They emerged on the headlands to discover the camp prepared just as Meda had described. The two tents were set as far apart as the headlands allowed. The larger one was backed up close to the forest boundary. Goods and weapons were stacked between the tents and the rest of the rocky pasture. The headlands' central rise formed a spine that ran from the forest to where the ridge descended to the river below. When the troopers set Dally's pallet down by the smaller tent, erected close to the Ashanta boundary stones, she could see nothing of the others.

The boundary stones marched down the steep slope and along the border of a broad meadow. The river was shallow enough for the rocky bottom to glisten in the fading light. The trail leading back to the Three Valleys communities was merely a dark line that ran along the river's nearside bank. To

Dally's left, beyond the stones, the headlands tumbled down to fashion the enclave within which the Ashanta city stood.

By nightfall Dally had regained enough strength to take a few tottering steps around the camp. But she did not assist in making dinner, for Connell would not allow it. She felt extremely uncomfortable having this handsome wizard serve her. And yet his presence carried a distinct solace. The guards came over long enough to help Connell fashion a fire pit and ring it with smooth cooking stones. They returned later with pots of stew and tea.

When Connell and Dally were alone again, he spoke for the first time since their arrival. "Your formal birth name offers a distinct curiosity."

"If it is indeed Dahlrin," she said.

"Is Dally a common name among the ladies of Three Valleys?"

"I am the only one so named, as far as I know."

"There you are." He spooned a bowlful of stew and passed it over. "You have no record of your family's heritage?"

"There might have been. But everything was lost in the fire that cost me my family." Dally scraped her bowl clean. "This is excellent stew . . . I'm sorry, I don't know how I should address you."

"Connell will do just fine. Certainly not 'master mage' or any such nonsense." Connell refilled her bowl. "Unless, of course, you're one of my acolytes and you've misbehaved. Then you can call me whatever you wish, but it will not help you any."

Dally accepted her refilled bowl. "Your students must love you."

"I don't see why. I'm quite useless as a teacher. I ask far more than I reveal. I make the most horrific errors in spell-casting. And I flee from the first hint of danger."

"I don't believe any of that." Dally set down her bowl. "Not for an instant."

"Eye of the tiger, heart of the mouse, that's me." He gestured toward her meal. "You won't finish that?"

"I am as full as I have been in quite some time," she replied. "And as content."

Connell poured her a mug of tea, then settled into his camp chair. In a companionable silence they watched the moon rise. Dally's heart sang at the thought of spending days in this remarkable man's company. And yet there was the lingering suspicion that he would prefer to be elsewhere. She stole the occasional glance across the fire. His face looked carved from some brooding golden stone.

She asked softly, "Why are you really here?"

He responded so quickly, Dally suspected he had waited all this time for just that question. "It is as I said before. The Mistress wishes for you to study with me. We will soon face the true enemy. Or so Meda thinks, and I agree."

She marveled at her ability to calmly respond. Which was a lie, of course. Her heart hammered at the prospect of spending long hours together. "The Milantian mage."

"Possibly more than one. Hyam and his company battled four wizards in Alyss. And before that they met with Milantian witches in a desert palace from beyond time as we humans count. Shona was there for both encounters—you should ask her about it." Connell glared at the fire. "One of those in Alyss was the witch who stole Joelle's breath. Their tactics were . . ."

"Terrifying," she guessed.

"Unexpected at every turn," he replied. "And yes. Very frightening as well."

"So you are to be my teacher," Dally said.

"Only if you like."

"Of course I like. But . . ."

"You wonder why the former head mage of the Emporis castle would stoop to teach one acolyte, and isolate myself here on the edge of a farming valley I only know of because Hyam was born here." He smiled at her across the fire. "The first reason is, your abilities are an astonishment. No human wizard in centuries has possessed the gift of far-seeing. Not to mention the blast you managed with the first use of your wand."

Dally had no idea how to respond.

Connell nodded, as though approving of her silence. "And then there is the second reason. You recall my mention of a certain Master Trace?"

"He leads the wizards of Falmouth."

"Very good. You listen. Unlike the vast majority of my students. Trace was the former Master of the Havering Long Hall and was the first to offer Hyam fealty. He urged Bayard, the Oberon earl, to send me to Emporis. I served there for a time as master mage, though my keep did not contain an orb of its own. Now I have been replaced by a certain young man who has proven to be a true adept. Fareed is also an excellent teacher. What is more, he comes from the desert people and so is a strong link to these tribes."

Dally translated that as, "You trained this young man as your replacement."

"Yes, well, whatever. And then Hyam was felled by this mystery illness, and we received the first rumors that the enemy was planning an assault on the Three Valleys. I don't suppose you've received an impression about why your home region was targeted?"

"No." Her breathing rasped in her throat. "Every time I even think in that direction, I am met by dread and the sense that he's out there, hunting me."

"Never mind. Turn away from that." His voice had sharpened enough to draw her back to the night and the fire. "Are you all right?"

Dally waited while her heart settled back into her ribs. "Yes."

"Good. I think . . ." Something turned him around. "We have company."

33

Connell rose from his seat and retreated back over the headland. When he reached the central rocky spine, he unsheathed his wand and spoke a word. Instantly the high ground was illuminated by a magical fire that bathed Dally with its warmth.

Bryna halted just inside the chest-high boundary stones, surveyed Dally's pallet, and asked, "You were wounded in the battle?"

"After," Dally replied. "When I received the next set of images."

"Will you tell me about them?"

"Yes," Dally said. "I will tell you everything."

Bryna carried a three-legged milking stool. As Dally described her images and how they assaulted her, Bryna seated herself. And listened in utter stillness. When Dally went quiet, Bryna said, "Your presence here tonight has split the Ashanta. It has brought the division among my people out into the open. And by doing so it has enraged some of our most powerful elders."

Dally did not reply.

"You recall what I said about the elders who oppose us and their tactics?"

"Each day they can delay your involvement is counted as a victory," Dally said. "I despise them."

"I do not have that luxury," Bryna replied. "But you are correct. For my opponents within the Ashanta community, each day we remain isolated and uninvolved in your battle—"

"It is not just our battle," Dally countered. "It is everyone's."

Bryna gave that a moment's silence, then continued, "They can pretend the crisis will remain beyond our borders. For one more day."

Dally did not know what she might say that would change anything, so she remained silent. Connell's light kept the night and the gathering chill at bay. What was more, she felt his presence as a soothing balm.

There was nothing to be gained by arguing with the striking young woman. Dally could not call her beautiful, though she was certainly pleasant to look at. Even so, her porcelain skin was stretched a little too tight, her features too stark, her eyes too blue. Everything about her was honed to its vital essence by the responsibilities she carried.

Bryna went on, "I have been expressly ordered not to come out and speak with you. And you have been forbidden from ever setting foot upon Ashanta soil."

"And yet you are here," Dally said.

"Because half of the Assembly wants us to go to the aid of our allies. Now. Before the next battle." Bryna's gesture took in the border, the headlands, the night. "Had you stepped inside, it would have been treated as an invasion. Your position here on the headlands, beyond our borders, has utterly flummoxed the opposition."

"I wish we could have met at a different time," Dally said.

"As do I."

"There is so much I want to ask you. So much I want to learn."

"And yet we must deal with the world as it is," Bryna said. "What is it you want?"

"I must speak with a dragon," Dally said. "This was the strongest image I have ever received. With it came two further instructions. I was not to reveal this until you and I met. No one among Shona's company is aware of this requirement."

If Bryna found this odd, she gave no sign. "And the second instruction?"

"We must first wake up a renegade Elf," Dally replied. "Hyam's life depends upon it. And mine."

34

Bryna's instructions on how they should proceed were not so much haphazard as incomplete. "You are asking me to condense five years of lessons into one midnight session."

"Only because we must," Dally said. She eased herself onto the pallet, glad for the chance to lie back down. Talking had never required so much energy. And her fear of what was to come had never been greater than now.

Bryna studied Dally in the glow of Connell's wand. What she saw must have caused her very real concern. "Why now? Why tonight?"

"Because if we don't," Dally replied, "Hyam will die."

"When, tonight?"

"No. I know because I asked. But very soon. That much was clear. Hyam's end may come at any time."

"And if we rush this, there is a very real chance that *you* might die!"

Connell called from his perch on the ridge, “Don’t take such risks, Dally. Not now, not ever.”

Bryna sighed. “He might as well bring his light in closer.”

Dally called, “Connell, please join us.”

Connell walked over, saying, “She’s right, you know. Give yourself time to heal and regain your strength.”

“And if Hyam dies, what then? Every image I saw without him led to defeat.”

Connell bowed to Bryna, then settled into his camp chair. “I still say you should wait. Rest. Prepare.”

Dally did not want to argue further. The temptation to give in was too great. The prospect of what was about to happen filled her with a dread so powerful she felt nauseous. So she asked Bryna, “What do I do?”

Bryna sighed again. “Close your eyes. Release yourself from your physical form. I will take us to your chosen destination. But before you do so, tell me again precisely where we are going.”

“First we need a translator.” Dally had no idea if she could even perform the task Bryna intended. Always before it had simply happened at the edge of wakefulness. All she could hope was that her weakness and fatigue might make it possible to do now, at this opposite side of sleep. “A desert trader whose heritage includes princely Elven blood was shown to me. His name is Jaffar.”

“I know of this one.” Bryna sighed a third time. “Very well. Let us begin.”

The desert merchant was not at all pleased when they invaded his slumber. He hovered there before them and demanded, "Is this a dream?"

Dally did not know how to respond. Bryna said, "In a way, yes."

"In a way." His expression was sour. "Are you real?"

"Yes."

"I mean, beyond this partial dawn."

"I know what you mean," Bryna said. "The answer is the same."

"You are Ashanta."

"I am."

"And yet you speak with me in the tongue of the human realm."

"Taught to me by Joelle."

"Ah. Joelle. She is gone, yes?"

"Her ashes now rest beside our offering stone."

Jaffar gave that the pause it deserved. Then he addressed Dally. "You are human."

"I am."

"Allied to the Ashanta."

Bryna replied, "She is. And hopefully my friend as well."

"So you have brought this human friend to me and interrupted my few hours of rest in the process."

"Actually, Dally brought me."

"What kind of name is that? And what is a human doing taking an Ashanta anywhere?"

Dally replied, "Hyam is dying."

The merchant's grumpy mood deepened. "I feared as

much. So it is not as the Elves claim, that he is merely weakened by his loss."

"It is more than that," Dally replied. "Much more."

"What does he suffer from, then?"

"That is why we came," Bryna replied.

Dally said, "We are hoping the dragon can tell us. And for that we need your help."

The dragon was nothing like what Dally had expected. Right from the very first words he uttered in that staccato drumbeat of a language, he astonished her. "I was afraid you would not come."

They met in a world of ice and rock. The sun was neither up nor set. The light was ethereal, the wind so fierce it shrieked in a thousand voices, turning every rock and icy crevice into a disharmonious pipe.

The three of them had traveled an impossible distance. They arrived in the endless twilight and stood there, overwhelmed by the brutal landscape.

Then a beast whirled down from the light-streaked clouds. Its wings held a diamond pattern designed to use the bleak world as a frame for its severe beauty. The dragon's wingspan seemed as big as Dally's village. He landed, gripped a rock with yellow talons, and uttered a single note. With that the wind was silenced, the world captivated by his presence.

This, Dally thought, was true magic.

The dragon's speech was a series of great booming

drumbeats. Dally thought if she had been there in true form, she would have been shattered by the power in each word.

Jaffar translated, "The king of his kind welcomes you to the land of ice and storm."

Dally asked, "You have been expecting me?"

When Jaffar translated, the dragon responded by folding his wings and settling down upon his talons. "I called and called. You heard me. At long last. I can only hope there is still time."

"To save Hyam," Dally finished.

"No, child of the valley. To save your kind."

Despite the grim tidings, Dally found it immensely comforting to know she had not been played like a puppet. "Am I human?"

"Hyam asked me the same question of himself. And he asked the mages. Then the Elves. And the Ashanta. *Who am I?* Over and over and over he asked. What benefit does the question grant him now?"

"The words of Mistress Edlyn leave me thinking the answer plays a role in my quest."

"Ah. That is different." The dragon extended his neck and leaned closer still, until all Dally could see was one gold-green eye. She wanted to ask if he was truly so big, where an eye was wider than she was tall. But for that instant she was held fast, the dragon's force capable of snuffing out her breath, her will, her thoughts, her life, if he had that desire. Then the instant passed and he leaned back, the pressure eased. "You are human. But there is a trace of something . . . The Mistress who awakens in you this desire to know your true quest, tell her she has great insight." He shifted around so that he could study her with his other eye. "You suffer from the same ailment as Hyam."

"What is it?"

"A magic I have never seen before, and cannot even name. Which is a mystery inside a mystery. My knowledge of magic is almost as vast as my years, and I am very old indeed."

"Every time I approach the Elven realm, I am assaulted by images."

The dragon gave a ponderous nod. "These are part of your quest and crucial to the victory of your kind."

"But each time I feel another part of my life is torn away."

"This should not be. Weakened, yes. But not splintered." He studied her anew, then said, "Ask the Elven rulers to share with you my tears. Hyam should be given the same."

Jaffar traded staccato words, then said, "I have informed the king that Hyam has not taken any sustenance for days. The dragon says he must be forced to consume the tears. They should grant him and us more time."

The dragon spoke again to Dally. "This journey you are making and our exchange will most likely impact you the same way. You may find it difficult to drink my gift. Nonetheless, you must."

"I will do as you say," Dally promised.

Bryna spoke for the first time. "This magic that has assaulted Hyam and my new friend. Is it Milantian?"

"Most certainly." The dragon's massive head shifted position. "I greet you, young Seer of the silent folk. And I thank you for your assistance."

"I have heard of your kind for years, since I began my training," Bryna replied. "My teacher spent her entire life yearning to meet you."

"And now you have fulfilled her wish," the beast replied. "You must make your leaders aware that others among your kind suffer from Hyam's affliction. It forms much of the opposition you face in aiding your treaty allies. Tell them the dragon king says that their hour of need is yours as well."

"I will do as you say, Majesty."

The dragon's gaze swiveled back. "What is your name?"

"Dally."

"From Dahlrin, no doubt. The past speaks to us through your name. Most interesting. Wait here." With that, the dragon stretched out his wings and disappeared.

She found it remarkable that such a massive beast as that could vanish and reappear without making a sound. He settled back upon his perch, tucked in the sail-like wings, and boomed the longest message of all. "You must traverse the Elven path once more. In this passage you will discover the next portion of your quest. Doing so will tax you to your very limit. Why you must be brought to the verge of your last breath, I cannot say. But it is so."

"If you do not know the task I must perform, why did you seek contact?"

"Because of the urgency, young Dahlrin. And the *partial* answer." He lifted his head and roared out his next message, a drumbeat that caused the neighboring hills to throw off their burden of ice and snow. "The Ancients spoke of a day of unity. It is upon us. Here. In this hour of direst need, you shall witness the realization of a promise forged in the time before time. The enemy seeks to divide you. But you must fight this."

"Unity," Dally repeated.

"Victory shall only be found through forging bonds stronger than the enemy's fury. Refuse to allow fears and old scars to keep you apart. And when this challenge is complete and the enemy vanquished, I invite you to return, Lady Dahlrin. I will welcome you. We will talk. And perhaps you will discover the mystery behind your name."

The dragon rose to full height. He blasted the sky with a stream of fire, then caused the earth to shudder as he beat the air with his diamond-patterned wings. He rose into the sky, his power defiant of the wind that once again shrieked about them. Despite the storm, still Dally heard the final drumbeat resonate through her being. A word that Jaffar did not translate because there was no need.

Unity.

The dragon blew flames a final time, and was gone.

35

When Dally returned, she rose to a seated position and stared up at the night sky. The air held a summertime cool. The moon had set, which meant it was very late. Somewhere in the distance a bird of prey screeched like a wounded child. Otherwise all was still. Dally knew she must go, but for a long moment she could not remember why. Just the same, she forced herself to her feet. The first person she saw was Bryna, standing on the boundary stones' other side. Waiting.

Connell hurried over. "Are you all right?"

"Fine," she replied. She smiled a welcome and said, "I need you to send for Ainya. Tell her I need the dragon's tears."

"I'm sorry, what—"

"This is important," Bryna said. "Pay attention."

"Tell her that Hyam must be forced to take a portion as well." When he started to turn away, she said, "Wait. Ask Edlyn and Meda and Shona to join us."

"Dally, it's the middle of the night."

"Shona said the next time I received an image, I was to alert her immediately."

When Connell had departed, Bryna said, "That was very smart."

"I must seek out what the images might show of our next step," Dally said. "Connell would never let me do what is now required."

Bryna watched her struggle to walk. "Are you sure you are up to this task?"

Because of what they had just experienced together, Dally told her the truth. "I dread it more than anything. And I'm terrified of what might happen. But you heard the dragon same as I."

In response, Bryna stepped across the boundary. "Let me help."

The two women slowly crossed the headland. The rocky pasture made for hard going, and Dally leaned heavily upon Bryna's frame. The Ashanta smelled faintly of some burned spice. "Do you use incense in your duties?"

"That is for later, yes?" Supporting Dally's weight caused Bryna to puff slightly. "You will come and see my home, and I will explain all such details."

"Will your elders allow it?"

"Of course, once we are successful."

"Unity," Dally repeated, finding great comfort in the word. Enough to fight down the terror at the sight of the Elven guards up ahead. She detected the first tendrils of power then, reaching out, ready to envelop and capture and consume another part of herself. "After it happens, you need to pull me back here. Away from the portal."

"I will do as you say." They took another step, then one more, and Dally jerked hard as the new images invaded her and blasted away the night.

The last thing Dally heard was Bryna's plea. "Don't die."

36

Dally lay on her pallet in a state that was neither asleep nor fully awake. There was a sweetness to her languor, as pleasant as the fragrance of a poisonous bloom. She was so very tempted to remain as she was, trapped inside the deadly fatigue. She was hungry to hold on to this toxic ease. Free from the pains she had known. Free from the loss of family and home. Free from the loneliness. Free from fear.

Free.

The whisper of invitation filled her with a siren's lament. Why bother with all that mess any longer? The cravings of life were meaningless and only led to more sorrow. She could stay here and do nothing. Accept that defeat was inevitable. It loomed there, directly ahead of her, as soon as she rejoined with the outside world. Enough with her futile efforts and all the pain such strivings had caused her. Life held no benefit. No reward. Nothing that justified the misery she had known, and would know again if she bothered to return.

Enough.

Yet there in the lure of surrender, Dally sensed a fire of rebellion.

The longer she focused upon this heart's light, the clearer Dally saw beyond her trapped state. For the first time she glimpsed a realization all her own, a purpose large enough to justify the hard life she had known. Here was an objective so gigantic, it made her years of lonely toil not just bearable but necessary.

She had *never* given up. Wept, yes. Ached and sobbed and experienced hardship, most certainly.

All for this moment.

So she might have the strength of will to defy the lure that had captured Hyam and sown dissension among the Ashanta. So that she might find the determination to move forward and take the next step.

Dally opened her eyes.

Connell's relief was so great he almost sobbed the words. "You're back."

Dally realized then that Connell held her hand. She looked around and saw Edlyn and Ainya and Shona and Bryna and Meda, all standing by her pallet and watching her with worried eyes. She realized the still air resonated with Connell's pleas for her to return to them.

Dally took a breath of secret triumph and said, "Help me up."

The dragon's tear was the vilest concoction Dally had ever been forced to swallow. They were not tears at all, Ainya explained, but the dragon's lifeblood. Hyam had collected it as it flowed from one massive gold-green eye. But the blood had coagulated since Hyam had sought to save Joelle's life. The smell rising from the vessel was rank, like putrid flesh. When Dally carved out a dark red morsel, it quivered on her spoon.

The noxious mess tasted worse than it smelled. Dally gagged, forced herself to swallow, and gagged again.

Connell was ready with a mug of tepid tea laced with honey. "I would say it serves you right, after sending me away like that."

Dally drained the mug, then sat there breathing hard, willing the liquid to stay down.

Connell observed, "You look better."

She nodded, not trusting herself to open her mouth just yet. Even so, she felt better already. A renewed energy surged through her body, warming her bones.

Connell said, "Your color is returning. And the fire to your eyes."

Dally looked at him. "I had no choice but to send you away. You would never have let me do what needed doing."

He looked like he wanted to protest, but conceded, "You're probably right."

What she wanted to say was, no one had ever said there was a fire in her gaze before. Certainly not a handsome young mage in a tailored uniform. Who gazed at her with such concern. "Thank you, Connell."

He had the most splendid smile. "For getting out of the way, you mean."

Edlyn was unable to hold back her impatience any longer. "Did you see what needs doing?"

"Yes, Mistress. I did." Reluctantly she tugged her gaze away and faced the women. "You're not going to like it."

37

They emerged from the Elven portal to a red and brooding dawn. The air was perfectly still. A ground mist billowed high enough to veil the sunrise in an uncommon gloom. The Elven gateway faced a forest road that was hardly more than a well-used trail. Beyond the road stretched a broad meadow turned palest yellow by the mist. The surrounding trees appeared as spectral wraiths.

Dally walked forward on tingling legs. She could still feel the force from three doses of the dragon's gift growing in her limbs, though thankfully the taste had vanished and her breakfast rested comfortably in her stomach. Dally thought the breathless quality suited her, as if the day was aghast at what they were about to attempt.

"That should be far enough." Ainya spoke a quiet word, and the fire emanating from her jeweled forehead vanished along with the crown. When Dally was released from the green veil, Ainya asked, "Are you all right?"

"Yes, thank you, Majesty."

Shona walked alongside the Elven queen. They were followed from the portal by Alembord and Connell and Edlyn, then the four dogs. Alembord and Connell were dressed in the rumpled uniforms of house servants. After that came an open wagon, followed by four young mages equipped with wands. These were led by Myron. The wizards were dressed as house guards, and their saddles bore the emblem of a distant hill fief. Four more soldiers, also garbed as house militia, followed behind them, leading nine riderless mounts. The Elven queen's aide blanketed all the horses with a spell. When they were well clear of the portal and Vaytan extinguished his magic shield, the horses snorted and tossed their manes.

Two of the troopers slipped ahead. One returned to report, "The road is clear. But not for long. We can hear wagons in the distance."

"Let's be off," Alembord said, and clambered aboard the wagon.

Ainya said, "Your plan is both simple and brilliant, young lady."

"She has the makings of a good leader," Edlyn said. The Mistress of the Three Valleys Long Hall was dressed as a matronly servant, in a pale grey dress with white trim, and a matching starched cap that flared her hair out like aging wings. "And a better strategist."

Dally had no idea how to respond. These good people were placing not just their hopes but their very futures in her hands. She was overwhelmed by all the possible fractures to her plans. She whispered, "I'm so afraid."

To Dally's astonishment, Shona said, "It is a sign of your maturing strength that you do not allow this fear to halt your actions." The young queen embraced her. "I do not have the gift of far-seeing. But I am confident nonetheless that you have pointed out the right path."

"Thank you, my lady."

When Shona released her, Ainya took her place. The Elven queen leaned forward and kissed Dally's cheek. "Farewell, dear one. Come back to us intact. You are too precious to lose, no matter how vital the quest."

The portal was well placed. Dally's company traveled several hundred paces along the well-used track. The wagon bounced and rattled as it slipped in and out of deep ruts. As they entered a deeply shadowed glade, Alembord hissed, "Form up. Tighter now."

The mages who had been granted wands were by far the most gifted of Shona's force. But for most of them, the two battles against the forest beasts had been their only real taste of conflict. They eyed the approaching woodlands with tight and fearful expressions, hands hovering near their sheathed wands. Connell drove the wagon while Alembord gripped a pike, serving as their lady's last line of defense. Edlyn was perched upon a padded seat that jutted from the wagon's rear corner. A quilted pallet covered half of the wagon bed, and Dally was laid out in regal comfort. Beside her were stacked an assortment of fancy boxes and chests, borrowed from Shona's belongings. Two of Alembord's soldiers rode ahead, two more at their rear. It was the maximum number any nobleman might reasonably send as guardians of a family member, even in such times as these.

But all Dally could see was the cloud-flecked sky and the tree limbs up ahead. “Stop here. I want to sit up. I need to observe what we are entering.” Which was only half true. The reality was, Dally had never been beyond the Three Valleys, and she was flushed with the prospect of seeing her first real city.

The group halted, her pallet was rearranged, then Connell asked, “Better?”

“Much. Thank you.”

At a word from Alembord, the company re-formed, and the two scouts went on ahead. When they gave the all clear, the group proceeded through the glade, around a sharp bend, and joined the main thoroughfare.

And what a road it was, paved in greyish-yellow stones and as wide as the river running through Dally’s home village. The forest was cut well back, such that the verge on either side was twice as broad as the road itself. This served as a resting place for numerous companies taking their leisure. Dally’s group was soon surrounded by the odors of roasting meats and the sounds of bleating animals. Dally could not take it all in. Nothing in her existence to this point had prepared her for the sight of so much humanity.

There were all manner of people. Greasy mendicants hawked their wares as they journeyed. A wealthy oil merchant rode within a gilded carriage while behind him stretched several dozen high-sided transports. Swarthy mercenaries from some distant sun-kissed land surrounded a coach with veiled windows. As they passed, one crimson curtain pulled back long enough for Dally to glimpse a dowager with a painted face and jeweled fingers. Then the curtain dropped, and the lead guard snarled at them to keep their distance.

Edlyn murmured, "My, but this takes me back."

"You have been to Port Royal, Mistress?"

"Never. But the road and the people." Edlyn took it all in with one sweep of her hand. "I was born to a half-caste woman before the main archway leading into Falmouth Port. Or so I was told. She died when I was still very young. I was raised by numerous aunties who served at the local taverns. They claim my father was a dashing guards officer who died stamping down a rebellion by one of the hill clans."

The two men on the wagon bench turned an ear toward Edlyn, and the mages drew their horses closer. Edlyn stared dreamily about, her eyes glistening. "My earliest memories are of the road leading into Falmouth, and the people, and the noise. The hill tribes are all at peace now, drawn together by the struggles that led to the battle for Emporis. They've sworn fealty to Oberon and to Shona. But in my childhood it was an entirely different story."

Alembord said, "I've heard tales of their savagery."

"That's true enough, I suppose. But they also held to their own brutal form of honor. And they were very kind to a young orphan girl. Especially once my abilities began to appear. I was six or seven at the time. For several years I brought in more than my share of trade. I learned to fashion pewter animals from the tableware and made them dance to the minstrel's tunes."

They were all captivated by the tale, drawn together in a manner that Dally could never have accomplished on her own. As she listened, she wondered if this was why Edlyn spoke as she did. Taking their minds from the danger up ahead, granting them a moment of unity and peace, however fleeting.

Dally asked, "How did you gain your freedom?"

"I wouldn't say I was ever a captive, not like the young years you've known," Edlyn replied. "I was born to this, remember. That roadside inn was the only home I'd ever known. Even after I moved into the palace caverns, I spent every free day back among my friends at the tavern. Watching the river of folk and animals. Hearing stories from beyond the first line of hills. It was a grand place for mysteries."

To Dally's surprise, Connell suggested, "And romance, perhaps?"

"Ah, well. It was so very long ago." Edlyn smiled at a passing squad of mounted troops. "What does an old woman know of romance."

38

They halted soon after, pulling into a broad wayside market sheltered by massive interlocking boughs. The day was growing hot, and the animals drank thirstily from spring-fed troughs. They bought food and took tables somewhat removed from the boisterous throngs.

Connell seated himself next to Dally and said, "Time for your next dose."

"No. Please. Later."

Edlyn added her voice to Connell's. The Mistress spoke gently, but it was an order just the same. "Drink."

Once Dally had gagged down another horrid spoonful of the glutinous mess, she did feel significantly improved. She was content to listen in silence as they ran through both strategy and timing. These were no longer her plans. The idea might have come from her, but as she listened to the others she felt as though she had merely planted a seed.

As Dally watched the road, she cast the occasional glance

at Connell. His closeness filled her senses. Dally had known several infatuations with local village lads. A dance or two at season fetes. A stolen kiss. A few whispered words. But all that seemed so distant now. This was her first contact with, well, a man. She had no idea what to do or say.

She wondered if Connell was this nice to all the ladies. The prospect stabbed at her. She wanted him to treat her differently than the others. And there had to be others, with a man this handsome and from a fine family and gifted in magic. No doubt his young female students had been madly in love with their strikingly grand instructor. Dally found herself jealous of them all. Logic had nothing to do with how she felt. More than anything else, right then she wanted him to see her as . . .

Special.

He turned and smiled at her then. Connell's eyebrows were golden in the sunlight, his smile both gentle and beckoning. Dally wondered what it would be like to kiss those lips, and blushed furiously at the direction of her thoughts.

Connell said, "Perhaps we should be going."

They exited the forest soon after. A broad vale expanded out to where hills rose to the left and right of the highway. Four other roads joined together here, forming a river of traffic and people streaming to and from the capital. The broad thoroughfare dropped gently down an emerald slope. Beyond stone barriers stretched a latticework of farms and crops and herds. All this was overlooked by grand manors that dotted the hilltops. And directly ahead of them rose Port Royal.

Far to their right, a grand lake nestled up against the city's ramparts, and from this flowed a moat that stretched out in both directions. The capital formed a gilded necklace strung around the realm's finest harbor. The city's walls gleamed a timeless yellow in the afternoon light.

A smallish island with sheer stone sides rose in the middle of the harbor, effectively splitting the port in two. An ancient fortress covered every inch of the island's flattened top like an ancient stone hat. There were numerous other palaces and grand estates inside the city walls, each nestled within a small island of green. The remainder of the city showed roofs and chimneys and towers, all of the same reddish-gold stone. The effect was as striking as it was uniform. Long streamers of smoke rose from countless kitchen fires, drifting cheerfully in the still air.

Alembord had once served a count who owned a Port Royal manor, and he described some of what they saw. "The fishing vessels are that motley lot clustered to the left of the customs fortress. The broad, flat expanse you see fronting the sea wall holds the daily fish market. To the right are the merchant vessels and warships."

"There are so many," Dally said.

"Hundreds," Alembord agreed. "Since the Oberons were deposed, the king has anchored his seagoing force here under his thumb."

The ships rocked gently with the incoming tide. The sea glistened beneath the cloudless sky. Now and then a larger wave buffeted the ancient sea wall extending from the two natural arms. The sound boomed like a distant cannon, echoing off the hills and frothing the old stone before falling away.

Dally asked, "Where is the king's residence?"

"Look there to the right. See the squared-off walls? That's the inner keep. The palace is below those six towers with the banners—that's the royal seal on the white backing. The king's emblem."

Dally asked because she had to. "And the treasury?"

Alembord cast her a worried look but merely said, "The large square windowless structure, just to the left of the inner keep's tallest tower. The only door is solid bronze and well guarded. It leads to a series of vast storerooms."

Connell said softly, "And where, pray tell, is the enemy?"

No one responded to that. But the answer hung heavy in the summer heat.

Everywhere.

39

Dally was overwhelmed by everything she saw. According to Alembord, the city, combined with the palatial estates atop the surrounding hills, was a day and a half's ride from end to end. Bright flags of office and fiefdom banners hung from numerous towers and rooftops. A faint breeze began to push inland, carrying with it the pungent odors of salt and sea and drying nets. Where the roads joined, a trio of minstrels stood by the rocky intersection and played a merry tune. Two jugglers with silver bells tied to their wrists and ankles tossed colorful balls in time to the music. Even so, all the faces Dally saw held a somber cast.

"These people look very worried," Myron said.

"Terrified, more like," Connell replied.

The city's main entrance was formed by a pair of massive gates, one inside the other. The broad moat separating them effectively made Port Royal an enormous island. Guards manned the first tower gate, inspecting wagons and exacting penny-sized bribes from everyone who sought entry.

Dally spotted a healer's assistant standing somewhat removed from the guards. She instantly knew what role he played. Before the thorn barrier had cut the Three Valleys off from the world, physicians often passed through plying their salves and their talents. Most tended to be cast-offs and second-rate medics who had never managed to gain a foothold in the more competitive cities. Others had fled their fiefdoms in disgrace. A few, though, simply loved the road. They all traveled with assistants or apprentices who were dressed as this one was, in tunic and leggings with the healers' logo on their hat and chest.

"Potions made up fresh with the finest of healing spells," he called in a bored voice. "Potions for the faint of heart and limb. My master is known far and wide for his ability to halt the wasting disease."

"The wasting disease," Alembord repeated, a bit too loudly, for it turned the man's attention their way.

He was portly and heavily jowled and showed them a greedy gleam. "What's this I see here? Another innocent lost to the wasting ailment?"

"Innocent, yes." Edlyn's voice was sharp in the manner of a servant who had spent years speaking for her mistress. "Lost, certainly not."

"And yet here you are, journeying to Port Royal in search of what my master can offer!" The apprentice was old enough to have grey in his hair. Which suggested his lack of abilities had kept him from ever gaining full healer status. "From where do you hail?"

Alembord responded in a voice that carried to the city guards who now observed them. "The hill fief of Reime. My lady is the count's only child."

"No doubt your local healers could do naught for her ladyship." The apprentice rubbed his hands together. "Just the sort of case my master specializes in."

The sergeant in charge of the gate's squad walked over. "There's a charge for all who seek entry into Port Royal."

A signal must have passed between Alembord and the apprentice, for the local man declared, "Three shillings per clan, that's the proper charge and not a penny more."

"Three shillings is twice what we paid last visit," Alembord protested.

"It's gone up to five," the sergeant snarled. "Difficult times, these."

"Three is the rate," the apprentice insisted.

The sergeant looked ready to argue, but Edlyn said, "Give the guard his due and let us be off. I want to see my lady bathed and rested. It's been a long journey." When Alembord looked ready to argue, she snapped, "Pay him!"

Alembord grumbled but did as he was told. As they were waved through the first gate, Edlyn said, "Now pay this good man his due as well."

Alembord pretended to seethe as he reopened the purse strings. The apprentice made the coin disappear, then asked, "Do you have lodgings?"

"We're to stay with the banker allied to the silent ones," Edlyn said.

"If the count's letter arrived," Alembord groused, slipping the purse back into his pocket.

"Hush now," Edlyn said, then addressed the apprentice. "Do you know the banker's residence?"

"All Port Royal know of that one," the apprentice replied. "But you'd be well advised to seek lodgings elsewhere."

"And no doubt be gouged by some flea-bitten innkeeper," Alembord muttered.

"That's enough," Edlyn said. "Good sir, we are well aware of the situation. But we have orders from our master. Will you show us the way?"

The healer's apprentice led them past the second portcullis and through a cobblestone market. Beyond the city's main stables, the avenue broadened and the houses became much finer. Here and there were tight patches of citified green, with carefully tended trees and splashes of summer flowers. The houses had crosshatched windows that masked their barred faces with diamond-shaped glass. Troops and armed sentries were everywhere. The city's atmosphere was tense, muted.

The farther they moved into the city, the quieter the apprentice became. Finally he halted at an intersection and said, "This watchtower belongs to the house you seek. The entry is up ahead on your left."

Edlyn asked, "What manner of man is he?"

"A good enough sort, by all accounts. Though I've never

met him. He is tended by another healer." The apprentice cast nervous glances to either side, then added, "The man and the people he represents are out of favor. That's a dangerous thing to be in these times. You're much better off finding another place to lay your head."

Edlyn paid his warning no mind. "Have your physician attend us tonight."

"Begging your pardon, miss. But the healer won't be coming here, oh my word no. Not for gold nor diamonds neither."

"Then give us his address."

"First house on the main market's eastern flank. Red door."

"Thank you, good sir. Alembord, give the man another shilling for his troubles."

The apprentice made the coin vanish, knuckled his forehead, and scuttled away.

Myron waited until the man was out of hearing range to say, "Perhaps we'd be better off doing as he said."

"Nonsense," Edlyn replied. "This location is ideal."

"The banker has maintained his loyalty to the Ashanta even when it's risked him everything," Connell said. "And the whole city knows it."

"The apprentice has just earned his coin," Alembord said.

40

The Ashanta banker's manor was enormous, a veritable palace set within its own keep. Beyond the front gates, a graveled lane curved beneath dual lines of fruit trees before arriving at a set of sweeping front stairs. The banker was away on some official duty when they arrived. The chief guard's name was Gert, and he greeted them with sour disapproval. But his master had been alerted to their arrival, the guard conceded, and so led them to the rear entrance. He clearly intended this as a slur, but Dally's one brief glimpse at the manor's formal rooms was enough. She insisted upon staying with her team. Gert snorted his disdain and stomped away.

There formed an uneasy truce between the banker's staff and Dally's team. Edlyn and Alembord made it work by simply ignoring Gert's suspicious jibes. The chief guard was a brutish man with scarred knuckles and a flattened nose. He spoke with a deceptively quiet voice, but Dally disliked how the rest of the house staff showed fear at his approach. Alembord despised the man. They said nothing to one another, but Dally thought it was like watching two cur dogs who waited for the chance to strike.

Edlyn insisted upon helping Dally up the stairs and out of her road-stained clothes and into the bath. The steamed water and the feel of clean clothes were exquisite. When they returned downstairs, they found a table laden with early-season fruit, a plate piled with smoked meats, a quarter-round of cheese, a clay pot of fresh-churned butter, and bread still steaming from the oven.

Gert stomped through the rear entry just as the cook's two helpers set out flat bowls of stew. The pair fled at his approach. He stood watching Dally and her company with eyes of dried mud, fists cocked on hips, a bruiser looking for his next conquest. As Dally felt the friction growing between Gert and Alembord, she shut her eyes, reached out, and signaled to her dogs. A few moments later, the wolfhounds padded in.

Gert took an involuntary step back and snarled, "Them dogs of yours better not give my lot trouble. Else I'll skin 'em and turn four dogs into one fine coat."

Edlyn and Dally and Alembord fed the dogs from their spoons. Edlyn said, "No trouble, Captain."

They were seated around a broad-plank table in a pantry as large as Norvin's cottage. Shelves held wheels of cheese and jars of spices and dough covered in cheesecloth and left to rise. The air was redolent with all the fragrances of a happy home. Gert's disagreeable presence was the only sour note.

The kitchen opened through the doorway directly opposite Dally's chair. Behind Dally was the boot room and weapons closet, and beyond them the passage leading to stables and storerooms and kennels and training grounds. The estate was rimmed by a high wall with guard towers set in each corner. The rearmost area of the yard held a vast kitchen garden and coops for chickens and geese.

Gert scowled in Dally's direction. "Don't think much of the banker's guests being back here in our space. Eating our food. Fouling the place with their dogs. Don't think much of that at all."

The cook was a rotund little man who glanced worriedly through the doorway and said, "The master left strict instructions . . ."

Gert shifted his glower, and the cook vanished. Gert shouted after him, "Where's my dinner?"

"Coming, coming, I wanted to reheat the stew, is all." He popped back into view long enough to add, "And let our guests eat in peace like the master said."

"Enough with the master. I know well enough what best suits his needs." Gert reached across the table, knocking Alembord's arm and causing him to spill a spoonful into his lap. "And what's needed is to have this lot back out on the street where they belong. Not here eating the master's food and bringing who knows what trouble to our doorstep." He gnawed off a hunk of cheese that dribbled crumbs down his front. "Uncommon strange it is, having his lordship order us to make room for the likes of you, no proper introduction, all in a rush, ordering me to ask no questions. Me, captain of his guard, commanded to mind you lot like I was—"

Gert stopped talking because he had suddenly lost the ability to draw breath.

Edlyn did not look around. "A bit of food get in the way, did it?" Her voice was mild, but not the least bit kind.

"Difficult to make trouble for others when you can't breathe," Alembord said. "It's a good thing the lady here has a hand in the healing arts."

The captain's fists rose to his throat, and he made a harsh gagging noise.

"I could probably help you," Edlyn said. She turned in her seat. "But in return we'd appreciate a bit of peace and quiet."

"A friendly welcome would be nice," Alembord said. He continued to feed spoonfuls of stew to his wolfhound. "Probably what your master ordered as well."

"Nod if you agree to our terms," Edlyn said.

Gert gagged and coughed and finally complied.

"That's a good lad. Now bend down here. I don't feel like getting up. I'm still enjoying this fine repast." When Gert did so, Edlyn touched his throat. "There. All better."

The guards captain coughed, hacked, and heaved a great breath. "You caused that, you did."

Alembord stroked his dog's ears. "If that's so, how wise is it for you to stand there and bait her?"

"Peace and quiet," Edlyn said. "A nice welcome. Pleasant words or none at all directed our way. That's the ticket." She looked up at him, and something he saw there caused him to step back. "And not another word about skinning dogs."

The banker entered the pantry just as they were finishing their meal. His name was Karsten, and he was every inch a patrician, with leonine features and strong limbs that defied his age. An abundance of silver hair swept back from a broad forehead. His glare was ferocious, his voice a resonant thunder. He took in the tableau with one swift glare, Gert standing in the kitchen doorway and spooning up the stew as he shot Dally's group venomous looks.

Karsten demanded, "Which of you is the Lord Reime's daughter?"

"I am, sir," Dally replied.

"Why are you back here with my staff?"

"I insisted. I do not wish to be separated from my company."

Karsten disliked it but did not argue. Instead, he gestured at his guards captain and demanded, "Is this man bothering you?"

"There's no problem," Alembord said. "Is there, Gert?"

Gert pointed at Alembord with his spoon. "Got the look of trouble, this one. He's nobody's house servant, that's for certain."

But the banker wasn't having any of it. "This woman's company are my personal guests. I left word to that effect with the night guard before setting out. What is more, the Count Reime is one of my most important clients. Which means they are vital to the future of this household."

Gert continued to scowl at the table. "None of us have

a future, if this lot's carting trouble with them. The streets are full of danger and woe—"

"Enough," Karsten snapped. "Their disposition is vital. Their well-being is vital. Their comfort and safety are . . ."

Gert scowled but conceded, "Vital, your lordship."

"Good. We understand each other." He turned back to Dally. "My lady, if you are quite finished, perhaps you will be so good as to attend me."

The banker's former chambers were palatial in size and décor. His offices covered a full five rooms, each grander than the last. He ignored the greetings cast his way by various clerks and assistants, and ushered them into his inner sanctum, a space larger than Honor's village hall. A senior aide and private secretary both entered after him and were genuinely shocked when Karsten sent them away.

When the door was shut, he said, "I have done as my unseen allies have requested."

"Demanded," Edlyn corrected. "The Ashanta made no simple request. They *ordered* you to help us."

He strode behind the massive desk and dropped frowning into his chair. "I would ask that you tell me why we are meeting at all."

Dally was accompanied by Edlyn and Alembord and Connell. They stood on a carpet woven with gold thread. The paintings adorning the side walls were ancient and very large. A tapestry covered the entire rear wall, depicting a group of nobles kneeling in fealty before a newly crowned king.

Edlyn repeated what Bryna had told them before their departure. "You served the last two Oberon kings. Your father and grandfather and his father before him. Your loyalty to the crown stretches back eleven generations."

"Twelve," Karsten said. "I make an even dozen."

"You survived the transition and helped to keep the Ashanta in their territories by agreeing to the new king's ultimatum. You forgave the debts owed to you by the Oberon realm. Forty tons of Ashanta gold. Lost."

"The new ruler threatened to strip the Ashanta of their territories, by war if need be. Territories that had been deeded to them by treaty a thousand years ago," Karsten said. "Treaties that should not be influenced by any transition of power within the human realm."

"You and the Ashanta both expected to recoup some of your losses by charging the new rulers a higher rate of interest," Edlyn went on. "But the crown has taken his business to other bankers. You have effectively been shut out."

"And you are certainly well informed." Karsten's piercing gaze was shadowed by his massive forehead, a brow made for frowning. "All that you have related is both secret and highly sensitive."

Edlyn's only response was to turn to Alembord and say, "Our lady should sit."

"Of course."

Karsten clearly disliked having control of his room taken over by this supposed house servant. Which was why Dally did not object as Alembord carried over a leather chair embossed with a royal seal. "Thank you."

Edlyn rested one hand upon the chair's back. "Because you represent a debt that will never be repaid, your remaining here in Port Royal places you and all your household under a very grave risk."

"And yet here I remain," Karsten said.

"Precisely."

He crossed his arms and scowled at them. "You are not from the House Reime."

"That is correct."

"You chose that fief as your supposed locale because it is so remote," Karsten said. "And thus would not be known by the city's militia."

"We did not choose anything," Edlyn replied. "As you well know."

He drummed his fingers on the leather-topped desk. "All right. I'm listening."

Alembord said, "The question is, who else might be doing the same?"

"This is the only room in the house where eavesdropping is forbidden."

"In that case"—Edlyn gestured to Dally—"allow me to introduce Lady Dahlrin, Seer to the Lady Shona, new queen of the human realm."

Dally stifled her protest. Though Edlyn had warned her that this would be required, she detested this elevation of her status. She felt as though her title and abilities, even this alteration to her name, were little more than loudly spoken lies.

Astonishment fractured Karsten's tightly assured gaze. "Can you offer some form of confirmation?"

"Alembord."

He crossed the room and extended one fist. In it rested Shona's personal seal. "Do you recognize this?"

"I . . . yes."

"Lady Dahlrin is here as the queen's personal representative," Edlyn said. "You will listen. And then you will obey."

41

Karsten did not take Dally's news well. "You want me to leave Port Royal?"

"You and all your household," Dally confirmed. "Tonight."

"But . . . what on earth for?"

Alembord remained poised by the massive desk. "Because if you stay, you die."

The banker studied the officer's grim resolve. "And you are . . ."

"Second in command of the Lady Shona's palace guard," Edlyn replied. "And this man here is Connell, former Master Wizard of Emporis, now serving on the queen's staff. And I am Mistress of the Three Valleys Long Hall."

Karsten paled. "Magic has been released into the realm?"

"It has been ever since the new king defeated the Oberons," Alembord said. "As you well know."

"Yes, of course, the dark forces, we suspected . . ." He searched the faces, one after the other. "Tonight?"

"If you go, you survive," Edlyn said.

Alembord added, "What is more, you can return in the company of your queen. In triumph. Once the dark forces now in control of Port Royal are vanquished."

He swallowed hard. "When will the attack begin?"

Dally replied, "The hour after dawn."

"At curfew's end," Alembord said. "While the city guard changes shift."

Edlyn said, "You must be well gone by then."

He fumbled with the arms of his chair, as if seeking the strength to rise. "What about my allies?"

They had discussed this long and hard during the trek into Port Royal.

"Every person you warn increases the threat of your capture," Dally said.

"And our defeat," Edlyn said. "You risk everything by telling the wrong clan."

"Family first," Alembord said. "And only those allies whose loyalty is beyond question."

Karsten rose in stages, his movements as guarded as an old man's. "I suppose I should begin."

"One more thing," Dally said. "I need a way to be transported through the city."

"We need to survey the field of battle," Alembord explained. "Lady Dahlrin needs to be seen as both an invalid and a woman of power."

Despite having this conflict brought into his home, the banker nodded and replied, "I have just the thing."

42

To his credit, Karsten was there to see them off. He indicated a pile of oilskins by his front portal. "A storm is coming in from the sea. You would be advised to carry these, unless your plans require you to return soaking wet."

Alembord asked, "Your house emblem is not to be found on them?"

"Credit me with a minimum of intelligence." Karsten indicated a wooden wheelchair waiting at the bottom of the stairs. "This was my late mother's. It should serve you well enough."

Dally quailed at the attention this would draw her way. But Edlyn said, "This is perfect. Again, our thanks."

"Weapons are expected of house guards these days." He pointed to the long staves stacked along the front wall. "These are the sort of pikes used by most city militia. You're certain you know where to find my family's healer?"

"I was stationed here for five summers," Alembord replied.

"Which clan did you serve?"

"House Laman."

"The count was a good man, and a friend." Karsten's scowl deepened as a line of empty wagons and carriages trundled through his front gates. A dozen household guards were saddling horses as Gert stomped about the side yard and shouted at all who came within range. Karsten said, "It is a shame I am now forced to share his ignoble fate."

Dally cut off any response Alembord might have made by stepping between them. "I and the next queen of the realm offer our heartfelt thanks."

His gaze remained locked upon the pending departure from his home and heritage. "And I'll thank you not to make this peril to myself and my family a vain effort."

The healer used by the banker's family was located at the point where the city began its northern curve around the harbor. As they left Karsten's compound, Alembord explained that the physician's location was ideal, as it granted them a reason to walk through the city's heart. The chair's wheels squeaked and clattered and announced their passage to everyone within hearing range. They took the most direct line, which kept them to fairly crowded lanes. They crossed a small market where some of the stalls were already closing down, as though racing the sunset. They were inspected by a number of patrols and household militia. Some glances were given to the size of Dally's team, but even this was not too unusual for such fearsome times.

The healer used by Karsten's clan was a potbellied man who clearly cared very little for his appearance. He wore a formal shirt whose right sleeve was stained with ink and a broad belt that did nothing to keep his gut under control. He peered at Dally from beneath a bird's nest of cotton-white hair. She liked him at first sight. His home was cheerful, the two apprentices who served him intelligent and anxious to please.

His inspection lasted all of ten minutes. "Wasting disease," he declared.

Edlyn was the only one of their group who had accompanied Dally into the healer's quarters. "You are certain?"

"No question. None whatsoever."

"And a cure?"

"None that work, madam. Nor even that might offer a small hope."

"We were told otherwise."

"One of those hawkers by the outer gates, no doubt." He made a note in his ledger, then used his cuff to blot the notations dry. "The healers they serve mix potions with gold dust and rare herbs. They bleed their patients and insist on daily steam baths in chambers filled with noxious odors from burning weeds. All this does no good whatsoever. A number of my unscrupulous colleagues have grown rich as a result of this disease."

Dally asked, "The ailment is widespread?"

"I see a dozen patients like you each day, my lady. More, now that the hill roads are free from the threat of snow."

"Do you know of anyone who has been healed?"

"Not even among those who have the gold and the influence to visit the royal family's own physicians. No doubt you heard that the Port Royal healers possess secret magical powers. I am sorry, my lady. I can offer something to ease discomfort. Nothing more."

Dally persisted, "Have you ever known an illness before when no one recovers?"

"No. And that's a mystery, I do admit."

Edlyn said, "So there's nothing you can do."

"We do not even know what it is, nor where it comes from, nor why it chose this particular time to attack. This city is as clean as it has ever been. There is no infestation of rats. Nor any ailment brought upon a plague ship. The water supply has been deemed pure. The air, the flocks . . ." He used both hands to sweep back his hair, leaving a blue stain upon his forehead. "I dread the numbers of hopeless cases that will arrive with the high summer. I've heard some towns now hold more afflicted than healthy."

"And yet some regions remain untouched."

"Aye, so I've seen with my own eyes. One town is filled with people who can scarcely drag themselves through another day, and the next contains not a single afflicted. They claim it's because of better air, lives better lived, they claim this, they claim that. I think . . ." The healer paused.

"Go on," Dally urged. "Please."

"There's a few ancient texts that speak of regions protected by convexes of hidden powers. Orb havens, they were called. What that means, I have no idea. But there are towns and even whole regions that remain untouched by the scourge."

"Orb havens," Edlyn murmured. "Now that is truly a marvel."

Dally asked, "What happens to such as me?"

The doctor's eyes glittered birdlike beneath his unruly hair. "My lady, it is not pleasant."

"I want to know."

"Very well, then, I will tell you. The plague's name says it all. The afflicted waste away." His expression was grave and sympathetic both. "The body's energy gradually slips out, as though it's sucked from the body. Some endure great pain, others none at all. Some have fevers, others . . ."

"Lie down and do not get up," Dally said, thinking of Hyam.

"Those who remain conscious lose all interest in food. They must be forced to even swallow liquids. And yet they do not die. They become half alive, entering a state that is neither asleep nor awake." He shrugged his confusion. "And then there are the most curious of all. Some of the afflicted begin to act and speak in a manner that is entirely different from anything they have ever done before."

"Angry," Dally said, thinking of the Ashanta elders. "Hostile. Treating others as though they were enemies."

"You have witnessed this?"

"From a distance, yes."

"This manner of affliction seems mostly to attack those in power, which is worrisome indeed."

Dally caught Edlyn's hand signal and said, "Thank you, good sir. You have been as helpful as possible, and more honest than most."

43

Dusk was gathering beneath a sullen sky when they left the healer. They lit oil lanterns supplied by Karsten's staff. The mages kept their wands well hidden and walked with swords clanking awkwardly from their belts. Alembord led them through winding streets, urging them to move swiftly, pressured by the coming curfew. The streets were mostly empty now. The only sounds of their passage came from boots scraping across cobblestones and the chair's constant creaking.

Alembord halted when a square watchtower rose above the last line of rooftops. "Here stands the farthest tower in this direction that remains flat to the wall. The next is where the ramparts make a sharp turn to the right. Each tower from then on is built into another corner."

Connell asked, "You know this how?"

Alembord pointed to his left, where the wall and rooftops began a gradual climb up a modest slope. "The count I served, his city residence was three towers farther along. Lovely view over the harbor from the top floors. That's how the city identifies the outlying districts, as each tower is numbered."

Edlyn said to Dally, "Tell us again what we seek. Everything you remember. The smallest detail."

Most of it she had said twice before. But Dally did not mind the repetition. "This is the only image I've had more than once. It's come three times. I stand before a tower rising from the city wall. The wall itself runs straight and true in both directions. As soon as the tower appears, I am filled with a sense of . . ."

"Rightness, perhaps," Edlyn suggested.

"More than that." Dally searched for the word and settled on, "Achievement. It is a triumph to be where I am. I know the tower plays some vital role in our gaining the prize. What that is, why it is important, I have no idea."

"Don't worry about what you can't explain," Connell said. "Give us the image and let us work through it together."

Dally liked his words almost as much as she did his smile. "The tower also is vital to our escape from the city."

"That I do not understand," Alembord said. "There are only three portals through the wall. And none of them open anywhere near a watchtower."

"I did not see how we left the city," Dally replied. "But in my images I stood before the tower twice. Once before we obtained the vial. Then again before we left the city."

"Maybe one tower has a secret hatch leading to the outside," Connell said.

"The city is known to be impregnable. No way in or out."

Alembord pointed down a narrow lane to where the city wall gleamed umber in the waning daylight. "Port Royal is not as old as Emporis or Alyss. But it was built in the same epoch. Those stones are bound in place by magic that has defied the ages."

"Just the same," Dally quietly insisted, "that is what I saw."

Edlyn said, "Then we will discover the means when we find the tower. Go on, lass."

"The wall to either side is flat and straight. No curve, as you describe. And no hill. I had the distinct impression that I stood with the city's main gates to my right."

"That gives us five towers, each five hundred paces apart," Alembord said. "We should—"

"One thing more," Dally said. "I heard a sound."

"You didn't mention that before," Edlyn said.

"I only heard it the last time the image appeared. And only for an instant. Now it seems as though it might have been why the image repeated itself. So I could hear that sound."

Connell asked, "What did you hear?"

Dally made a rushing sound between clenched teeth.

"Wind, perhaps," Alembord said.

"No. Of that I am certain." She pointed at the cobblestones. "It came from below. And when I heard it, the earth trembled. Like it was afraid of what was about to happen."

44

They took a series of residential lanes that ran parallel to the city wall. Alembord assured them they would attract far less attention by not walking directly alongside Port Royal's first line of defense. The next tower they passed was clearly defined against the growing dusk. They walked down an alley to where Dally had a clear view. She studied it and remained silent. To speak at all risked giving voice to her fears that she would miss whatever signal she had been intended to pick up on. Finally she shook her head, and they went on.

The wind gradually picked up, moaning through each side lane and carrying a damp, salty fragrance. Dally worried that the noise would keep her from hearing anything that might rise from beneath the stones. Her doubts magnified as they passed the second tower.

The ancient stone bastions were set precisely five hundred paces apart. As they approached the third, a blustery shower blew in from the sea, pelting them with a stinging rain. Dally bundled farther into the heavy oilskin cloak, drawing it over her head. But she dropped it down again because it muffled all sound.

Then . . .

"Stop," Dally ordered. "This is the one."

There was nothing to distinguish that particular tower. The same watch fires glinted off the guards' helmets. The parapet gleamed like a wet stone cauldron.

Alembord pointed to a pair of troopers patrolling the wall to their right. "We can't stay here."

Edlyn said, "Myron, you and everyone else, step into the nearest side lane. No, Connell, you need to stay. Dally, can you stand?"

She was already rising. "Yes."

"Take her chair. Go. Hurry." When it was just the four of them, Edlyn said, "Go on, lass. Take your time."

"Time is what we don't have," Alembord fretted.

"Hush now. Go on, Dally."

Connell hovered close enough for Dally to feel his breath upon the back of her neck. But he did not touch her. She took a step, listened. Nothing. Another step. Edlyn drew Alembord farther away from the tower, over to where they were partly blocked from view by a residence's front portico. Dally continued to walk slowly, a wavy path that took her ever closer to the tower. She heard the soldiers' soft voices from far overhead. Which was remarkable. She would have thought her heart was thundering far too hard to hear anything.

Then she sensed it. "Here."

Connell stepped closer still, his body tense against her side. They stood like that, locked in silence, listening with every portion of their beings. Then he wheeled about, hissed, and motioned.

Edlyn and Alembord slipped forward. Almost instantly, Edlyn murmured, "Oh my, yes."

Alembord asked, "You hear something?"

"I do indeed." She gripped the captain's arm and drew him closer. "Don't listen with your ears. With your *boots*."

"I don't . . ."

They clustered there in a tight group for a pair of excited breaths. Dally could smell the smoke drifting down from the watch fire. She heard the scrape of troopers' boots upon the stones overhead. There was the clank of metal, a weapon scraping upon the wall. None of it mattered. Not even the strain and fatigue she could see on these three faces. They had moved so fast, pushed so hard. So they could stand clutched together as a single unit. Here. In a storm-drenched city street, a few moments before the nightly curfew, listening to something that rushed and whispered softly beneath their feet.

Dally did not know what it meant. Nor at that moment did it matter. Simply having this affirmation of her image granted her an instant of genuine hope. That her life had a new meaning. That she was right to put these good people in such peril. That she had been correct to do as the image had shown, and send a banker away from his family residence. That there was indeed a chance, however slight, that they might strike a blow against a foe who had robbed her of home and family and life.

Edlyn whispered, "You hear it."

"Yes, but . . ." Alembord bent over as if seeking to hear what could not be heard. Only felt. "You know what that is?"

"Oh, without question." She pulled at his sleeve. "Let's join the others."

Together they moved over to where they were blocked from view. Alembord asked, "Is it really so important?"

"It's more than that," Edlyn replied. She pointed back across the empty rain-swept avenue. "That is a sign we might all survive tomorrow."

45

They hurried away from the tower. The young mages took turns pushing Dally's chair. Connell and Myron and Edlyn and Alembord walked several paces ahead, driven by the pending curfew.

They moved at scarcely less than a trot. Dally's vision shook from their rattling pace across the cobblestones. But she could see the four officers clearly enough to know they were making plans. Because of what they had just discovered. Because of Dally. And a dragon none had seen, save her. They trusted her with their lives. And, truth be told, with the realm's future. The prospect of what was to come left her both thrilled and terrified. Even so, as long as she kept her gaze fastened upon the four striding ahead of her, she knew a faint shred of hope.

They angled slightly away from the banker's house. One of the young mages muttered a question but was hissed to silence by his mates. Alembord kept to the side streets now.

The wind picked up momentarily, blowing in a fitful squall, and she tasted the sea on her wet lips. They scurried into a tight alley and halted when the inner keep rose directly across the intersection.

Alembord said to Dally, "Tell us again what you saw in your dream."

She had assumed that was the purpose behind their detour. "It wasn't a dream. It was another . . ."

"Event," Edlyn supplied. "That is how the ancient scrolls describe what the far-seers report. Events that change history."

"I was shown a windowless chamber," Dally said. "The biggest room I have ever seen. Filled with every manner of treasure. Chests of gold and jewels both."

"Then our objective can only be one place." Alembord pointed across the street to where the inner wall rose as high as a man-made cliff. "Directly opposite us is the royal treasury."

Connell asked, "You have been there?"

"Twice, but only so far as the entrance. After the new king was crowned, the fief holders were required to bring their gifts here. It was intended as a humiliation, one of many. The king was not even present. Some lackey made a recording of what was offered and who brought it."

Edlyn asked, "What did you see?"

"Just as Dally described. A vast, windowless hall filled with treasure. And other chambers opening to either side." He shook his head, a sharp jerk that cleared away the rain. "What a waste."

Edlyn asked, "Lass, was there anything else?"

"The vial holding Joelle's breath was on a shelf."

Alembord demanded sharply, "You're certain that was what you saw?"

"I am." Dally felt pushed away by the strength of Alembord's wrath. "Why does that anger you?"

"Because," Edlyn replied, "it means the evil one has taken control of the realm's wealth."

Connell said, "Describe the vial again."

"The size of my hand, perhaps a bit longer." She held up her first two fingers. "As narrow as this. It looked to be solid gold, but I can't be certain of that."

"Purified gold has a unique ability to contain a magical force," Edlyn said.

"There was writing on both sides, in a tongue I did not recognize. Nor did it matter. I knew what it was the instant I saw it." She paused in case they wanted to question her certainty. But when they remained silent, she went on. "The vial was supported by a thin circular frame, like a crown. The frame was made of gold wire set with emeralds."

"That sounds distinctive enough," Connell said.

Alembord gave another angry jerk of his head. "You do not know what you are saying. That front chamber could hide a hundred such vials. A thousand. And there are more chambers besides. We could hunt for years and not find it."

"I have an idea about that," Dally said.

Alembord's next question was cut off by the tolling of many bells around the city. Connell hissed, "The curfew."

But as they started away, Edlyn jerked to a halt. She ignored Connell's urging whisper and stepped away from the shadows, into the intersection. There was no one in the broad avenue fronting the wall, not even a sound. But she stood there, ignoring the rain, staring up.

In the light of their lanterns, Dally saw Alembord's face become so grim he looked almost haggard. "What is it?"

"The locals call this Birdcage Walk," Alembord said.

Edlyn turned around and murmured, "The rumors are true, then. Of how the new king punishes those who offend him."

"They are not rumors," Alembord replied.

Dally felt drawn by equal parts dread and a sudden need to know and understand. She walked over and stood beside Edlyn. And moaned, "No, no, no."

Cages and nooses were strung from the high ramparts. Dozens of them. More.

Dally sensed the others joining them. She heard several of the younger mages sob. She knew it was not just pain for those suspended overhead. They feared that if they failed tomorrow, this was the best fate they could hope for. Strung up along the inner keep's rear wall.

But Dally was not frightened. The sight made her angry. Furious, in fact. She said, "This has to be stopped."

"That," Alembord said, "was the reason I left my home fief and journeyed to Falmouth Port and joined the count's forces and swore fealty to the new queen. So that I could return and stand here with you."

Dally wiped away rain turned hot with her tears.

"Even if we have only half a hope," Alembord said, "we

must give it our all. We must show the enemy that the time is not theirs. Nor the city. Nor the lives within our realm."

Connell placed his hand upon Alembord's shoulder. "It is good and right to stand in your company."

Edlyn cleared her face with both hands. "We must be away."

46

They took rooms on the manor's top floor, formerly occupied by the now-departed servants. The ceiling slanted where the roof descended, and the windows were tiny. All four wolfhounds were settled in a separate bedchamber. Dally would have preferred to keep them with her, but there simply was not room. As it was, she and Edlyn could only pass one another by turning sideways.

Dally endured another dose of the dragon's elixir, bathed, and was brushing her hair when Edlyn emerged from the bath. Dally stood before a tall chest of drawers, watching her reflection in an age-spotted mirror. All the room's furniture held a rough-hewn quality. The beds were narrow, the carpets threadbare. But the room was spotless and smelled of recent cleaning.

Dally had seldom seen her reflection, and never for very long. Her hair when freshly washed tended to spring out in every direction, so a vigorous brushing was required. There was a reassuring normalcy to be found in the action. Her mouth still held the pungent flavor of her latest dose. She was tired, yes, but she knew her strength was returning. And tonight she was especially glad for the chance to stand there and study herself. She disliked the taut skin over her cheeks and the feverish glint to her gaze. But they suited the moment. She felt both calm and frantic. She looked famished, which she was in a way, but not for food. She desperately wanted to lie down and rest, enjoy a languor that might last for days, even weeks. But it was not going to happen. Instead, she faced the prospect of another short night, and then . . .

Dally gasped and jerked back. The mirror no longer showed her reflection.

Edlyn demanded, "What is it?"

Dally heard Bryna's voice, though the Ashanta Seer's lips did not move. "Can you hear me?"

"Yes."

Edlyn asked, "Yes, what?"

Dally gripped Edlyn's robe and drew her over to where she could see the mirror's surface. The older woman echoed Dally's indrawn breath.

"Good," Bryna said. "I have been contacted by our friend. Wait there."

Swiftly Dally explained to Edlyn what she had heard.

They stood there together. Two faces full of anxious expectation. Finding strength in the company of a trusted friend.

Waiting.

When Bryna returned, she glanced at Edlyn and asked Dally, "Can she hear me?"

"No."

"Greet the Mistress for me. Tell her I wish I was standing beside you both."

When Dally relayed Bryna's words, Edlyn replied, "You are precisely where you need to be just now. As close as you are permitted to approach. For the moment, that is enough."

Bryna smiled her gratitude and asked, "Can you find two more mirrors?"

They rushed down the hall, pounding on doors, and returned as swiftly as possible. Connell was with them now, and Myron and Alembord. They gaped at the woman watching them from the right-hand mirror.

Alembord demanded, "What—"

"Silence, all of you," Edlyn commanded. "Dally, can she hear me?"

"I can," Bryna replied. "These are all trusted allies?"

"Our lives and futures depend upon one another," Dally assured her.

"Very well. Let us begin." She vanished for a moment.

When she returned, Jaffar's familiar scowl filled the second frame. "What nonsense is this?"

"It is nothing of the sort, and you know it," Dally replied. "It is good to see you."

"I suppose if I must have my sleep disturbed, it's not altogether bad to be woken by a beautiful young lady." He waited, then demanded, "Aren't you going to tell the others what I said?"

"Certainly not." To the room she said, "This is Jaffar. He is—"

"Mayor of the hidden desert enclave called Olom," Alembord said. "A renegade Elf. A desert caravan merchant. And a scoundrel."

"I heard that," Jaffar said. "Greet the rogue for me."

When Dally passed on the message, Alembord replied, "I wish you were standing here beside me. We could use your eye and blade both."

"Where are you, then?"

"Inside Port Royal," Alembord said. "Crouched within the enemy's shadow."

"He is there?"

"We have seen nothing, save fear on every face," Edlyn replied. "Come sunrise, we will know for certain one way or the other."

Jaffar demanded, "How large is your army?"

"All such discussions must wait," Bryna interrupted. "Our ally is growing impatient."

She vanished, and when she returned once more, the entire room cried with shock. For there in the third mirror stood a dragon. Or part of one. He remained at some distance, but even so he could not fit his entire head into the frame. He shifted back and forth, inspecting them first with one eye then the other as he chattered.

Jaffar said, "The dragon greets you and is glad to see you are still alive. He was uncertain you would survive this long."

Edlyn replied primly, "We are harder to kill than we may appear."

"Let us hope our enemy feels the same way," the dragon replied. "I greet you, Mistress of the Three Valleys orb. It is good this young one can rely upon your wisdom and guidance."

Edlyn bowed low. "All my childhood dreams are now alive before my eyes, good sir."

The dragon allowed Dally to introduce her company and offered gallant words to each in turn. When it was Alembord's turn, the dragon said, "I am very glad to see you again, Captain, serving this company in their direst hour. You represent the finest of human virtues. Stalwart in the face of odds you understand better than all the others combined. Courageous when you have every reason to fear. Armed only with steel when you know the enemy can melt your weapons with a glance. Loyal to a queen who has no throne. Trusting the guidance of an untrained woman because others call her an adept. I salute you."

Alembord bowed, his jaw clenched tight. "You do me great honor, lord."

"When this is over, we must meet. Tell Hyam I said as much. Or the Elven queen."

"I shall cherish that as a reward and honor both, my lord."

The dragon then turned to Dally and announced, "I have uncovered spells ancient as the wind. I think they may help you in your quest."

47

The day started with no real dawn at all. Dally had never before witnessed a storm off the sea. The tempest carried a powerful energy. Every breath filled her with a sense of possibility. Even while her mind remained caught by so many fears, her body was growing ready for the next step, the coming battle.

When she came downstairs, she found Connell and Edlyn crouched together at the long pantry table, their heads bent over a diagram Connell had drawn upon a scrap of parchment. Edlyn had pushed back the dark by lighting the kitchen's every candle and lantern. Otherwise the downstairs rooms were silent and cold. Myron arrived next and used a puff of magic to start the kitchen fire. Dally found it comforting to go out into the rain and hunt about the empty chicken coop for a few forgotten eggs. There was so much danger imbedded in the coming hours, so many harsh choices. Collecting eggs was a very familiar task. It reminded her of how far she had come, from a lonely kitchen wench to a woman with purpose. And friends. And a future. Perhaps.

Dally returned to the kitchen and gave Myron the fourteen eggs, then Connell greeted her with another dose of the dragon's elixir. When she had forced it down, he said, "You are looking much better."

"I feel it."

As he turned away, he added, "And more beautiful."

Dally wished she knew what to say. How to respond to such an unexpected gift. But all she could do at that moment was smile.

Alembord came in while they were making tea and slicing bread. He shook the rain off his cloak and hung it by the fire. Edlyn handed him the first mug of tea and asked, "Did you find what you sought in your nighttime wanderings?"

"I did indeed."

Edlyn glanced over to where Dally was laying out cheese and salami and great clay jars of pickled vegetables. "Then there is hope on this grim day."

Dally wished she could share Edlyn's optimism. She wished she could see beyond the coming assault to a time of safety and peace. But just then she found it necessary to retreat from their talk of strategy and attack and escape. She saw how fear tightened the young mages' expressions and knew she probably looked the same.

Connell waved her over. "Come join us."

She sat beside him and stared out the open rear door. She found it astonishing how a simple squall could erase the summer morning. The wind carried a wintry chill and the light was dismal. The empty rear yard only added to the sense of peril and dire endings.

"What a fine beast," Connell murmured. The words drew Dally back around. Connell was slicing sausage with his knife and feeding every other bite to her unnamed wolfhound. "I have never seen such a mix of beauty and strength."

Dally watched the man more than the dog. She saw Connell's innate goodness and quiet strength.

Connell set down his knife and stroked the dog's white streak. "They are ferocious, yes?"

"Norvin has seen one smaller than these bring down a full-grown bear."

"Norvin is . . ."

"The mayor of Honor," Dally said. "A good man. His dogs are known far and wide for their intelligence and their loyalty."

Connell picked up his knife and sliced another piece and gave it to the dog. "I believe it."

"Connell." She took a breath. "This dog is yours."

Dally had no idea others were listening until all movement ceased, all chatter.

He lifted his gaze. "Dally . . . are you sure?"

"I am. There is a rightness to this."

Edlyn settled a hand upon Dally's wrist. "There is indeed."

After breakfast they entered the home's deepest cellar and recharged their wands. Port Royal was located over a very strong juncture of power. As they worked, Edlyn described how the city had once been the capital of an empire where magic was a component of everyday life. Port Royal was supposedly not as old as Emporis, she explained, but after so many centuries it hardly mattered.

They set off soon after. They all wore their warrior mage uniforms beneath oilskin cloaks taken from the guard station. Alembord and his four guards carried the same long pikes as the city patrols. Myron handed traveling lanterns to his mages but did not light them. Those were for later.

They halted by the manor's outer gates. Alembord surveyed the group and said quietly, "For Shona."

"Queen of a realm soon to be released from shadows," Myron said.

"Leader of a people she will help make free to hope again," Connell said.

"Where magic is used to foster the people's lives and futures, and release them from the unseen burden," Edlyn said.

They waited then. Dally felt the fear clench her entire frame, but she knew she needed to add her voice to theirs. She managed, "Where the races of this world are united and at peace."

Alembord unlocked the outer portal. He pointed his wolfhound over to Dally. She expected him to make a request then—to keep his animal safe, bring it back—and she dreaded hearing the words, for she had no intention of starting such a perilous day with a lie.

But Alembord merely said, "To your stations. Wait for our signal. Do your duty to the best of your ability. Then we gather at the meeting point. Now go."

48

Dally walked with Connell and Edlyn. Nabu and Connell's wolfhound padded ahead of them. Alembord's and Edlyn's dogs took up the rear. Dally found the odor of their wet, feral heat a comfort. Connell carried a long coil of rope, while Edlyn had a leather satchel containing food and the dragon's elixir slung from her shoulder.

The curfew was still in place, so they kept to side streets as much as possible. Twice they spotted squads marching down the larger avenues. Which meant their timing was perfect, according to Edlyn. Soldiers weary from guarding a wet wall through an empty night were being replaced by guards drawn from their warm, dry beds. There was always a bit of friction at the change of shifts, a few minutes of confusion and too many bodies crammed along a narrow passage. Some would be impatient, others reluctant, everybody cold and wet. Perfect.

When the inner keep came into view, Edlyn began searching for the house Alembord had identified. She quietly tested each doorknob in turn, then walked on to the next. Directly ahead of them loomed the wall of the inner keep. And beyond that, unseen from their vantage point, stood the royal treasury. Watch fires gleamed from the ramparts, their light ruddy and feeble against a dawn that refused to appear. Dally watched Edlyn try yet another door and listened to her heart beat as fast as the falling rain.

"Here," Edlyn said, and shoved open the portal. "Inside."

The front of the house was one large room, with a long counter running a few paces removed from the left wall. The chamber smelled of flour and old bread and disuse. Behind the counter rose a pair of huge baking ovens. The building was cold and dusty and dark. But at least it was dry.

Edlyn told Connell, "Alembord found stairs to a deep cellar in the back room. Go make sure we're in the right building."

Connell left and soon returned, bearing a battered pail that splashed as he walked. "The stairs are there. And a hand pump that still works."

The waiting was not as difficult as Dally had imagined. Edlyn unpacked her sack and prepared a second breakfast. She said, "Dally, take the dragon's elixir. Then we should eat."

Connell watched Dally shudder her way through another dose, then handed her a ladle filled with fresh water. He told Edlyn, "I am far too frightened to eat anything myself."

"Oh, hush your nonsense." She passed him bread with cheese and sausage. "There is no telling when we might have another calm moment."

"Did Alembord sleep at all?" Connell asked.

"A few hours, perhaps." She gave Dally her portion. "Alembord is a warrior. He has been trained to go without sleep. And food. And the slightest hint of safety. And still be ready for battle."

Dally asked between bites, "Did Alembord find another house for his team?"

"A private residence directly across the main avenue from your tower," Edlyn replied. "It appears there are empty buildings everywhere in Port Royal. Another symptom of the realm's diseased state."

Edlyn handed around portions, which they fed to the dogs. Connell observed, "You sound almost happy."

"My entire life has been spent under the enemy's shadow," Edlyn replied. "It is good to be taking the initiative."

Dally asked, "Despite all the risks?"

Edlyn smiled as she fed a slice of sausage to Alembord's wolfhound. "Your plan is a good one, lass. Never fear."

"Our plan," Dally corrected. "It's yours as much as mine now. Maybe more."

Edlyn stroked the dog's silver fur. "Not long now."

As they waited for the bells to announce the end of curfew and the changing of the guard, the rain abruptly intensified. Water began falling in an almost constant sheet. Dally opened the front door and stood watching the sight. Edlyn and Connell walked over and joined her. The rain fell so hard they could not see the buildings across the narrow lane.

"This is not a natural storm," Connell said.

"No," Edlyn agreed. "This is marvelous."

Dally asked, “Do you think the dragon is behind this?”

“If so, you must hug him for me the next time you meet,” Edlyn replied.

Dally tried to imagine embracing a beast whose left eye was larger than she was. Then somewhere in the distance, a bell began to ring. And another. More and more bells tolled softly, almost lost to the rushing water. The sound was as feeble as the dawn light.

Edlyn said, “We should begin.”

49

The rear of the bakery was split into living quarters and a far larger workspace. Rain blanketed the barred rear window and drummed hard on the roof. The cellar door was where Alembord had said, thick and oak and bound by iron strips. As Edlyn lit her wand, Dally's senses were filled with the fragrances of clove and cinnamon and mint. They descended into a cellar carved from bedrock. When Dally's foot touched the stone floor, she felt as well as heard the drum of rushing water from below. Both the sound and the vibrations rising through her legs were much stronger here, inside this underground storeroom.

Then in the distance, louder than the bells and rain, they heard a rolling thunder.

Edlyn rubbed her hands together in undisguised glee.

Connell said, "Shouldn't we . . ."

Edlyn held up her hand. *Wait*.

Dally stood there, panting in time with the dogs.

Then Edlyn said, "What do you hear?"

"Nothing," Dally replied, for the sound of rushing water was gone now.

"Precisely," Edlyn said. She shifted over to stand in the center of the cavern. "Dally, take the dogs and stand well back. Connell, apply your hottest flame to the floor."

They bored a hole through the stone. Twice Dally offered to help, and both times Edlyn ordered her to stay back. The second time, Connell looked up long enough to grin and reply, "We're after an opening, not a blast that might well take down the house."

"Pay attention to your work," Edlyn snapped, drawing him back around.

The floor glowed red-hot, turned molten, and fell into the depths below. Dally ordered the dogs to stay, stepped forward, and peered through the opening. The liquefied stone briefly illuminated a cavern broader and higher than the cellar, then hissed softly when it touched the distant floor and went out.

Edlyn paused long enough to tell Dally, "Go back upstairs. Check on everything, lock the front door as best you can, and shut the cellar door on your way back."

The rain fell even harder now. It drummed upon the roof like a waterfall. In the distance, Dally heard faint screams and shouts.

When she returned to the cellar and reported, Edlyn said, "Do be sure to thank the dragon for us."

"We're ready," Connell said. "Dally, come tell me if the dogs can survive such a drop."

He turned the wand's gemstone into a beacon, then directed the light down into the hole. Dally leaned over, the stone edge still hot through her wet shoes. "Yes."

"Are you certain?" Connell's head came down close to her own. "It looks very deep."

Edlyn joined them and said, "I suppose we could rope their chests and lower them one by one."

"There's no need," Dally said. Far below, trickles of water illuminated the stone floor. "I once watched a wolfhound jump down from the roof of the village hall."

Connell straightened and said, "We'll lower you first, then send the dogs down one at a time."

The rope lashed to Dally's waist ground softly as it slid over the hole's rough edge. She could hear Connell and Edlyn huffing from the effort. She landed with a soft splash.

Edlyn said, "Draw your wand and speak the words I gave you. But softly, softly. We are simply after a little light. Then tell us what you see."

She did so, then replied, "A huge empty tunnel that goes on forever in both directions."

"Splendid," Edlyn said. "Now call your dogs."

Once the four wolfhounds were safely down inside the tunnel, Connell lowered Edlyn by himself, then anchored the rope and slid down. He splashed in the water puddled along the floor, then examined the tunnel. "Well."

"Well indeed," Edlyn agreed.

"I had suspected we'd all be dead by now."

"You thought no such thing," Edlyn chided, but in a good-natured tone. She paused as a scream echoed from far overhead, loud enough to be heard above the sound of falling rain.

"Not long now," Connell said.

50

According to Edlyn, in the city's earliest epoch, back when magic was considered a vital component of everyday life, it was decided that a river flowing through the city's heart ran the risk of flooding the streets. So the river was diverted underground. It was a feat of engineering skill and magical design, one that required dredging a lake outside the city walls, then burrowing a gigantic tunnel from one side of the city all the way to the sea. The tunnel was designed so as to flow directly beneath the inner keep, granting the palace a constant and unending supply of fresh water.

And then, over time, the tunnel and its history were forgotten by all but a few mages with access to the oldest of scrolls.

Alembord and Edlyn's plan was devastatingly simple. Block the tunnel. Halt the flow of centuries. Grant Edlyn and Dally and Connell access to the royal treasury from the one direction no one might suspect—underground.

And by flooding the streets, they hoped to create enough havoc to escape.

Edlyn said, "All right, my dear. Time to try the dragon's first spell."

"Perhaps you should cast it," Dally replied.

"Stuff and nonsense. The dragon made them a gift to you personally."

"Dragon spells," Connell said. "This conversation is drawn from my earliest legends."

Dally said, "You heard the dragon same as me."

"Actually, we only heard what you repeated to us," Edlyn replied. "And that was intended as backup. We all know of your astonishing abilities with spellcraft."

"I only know two spells."

"Three," Connell said, pointing to the light still streaming from her wand.

"Four. Let's not forget your recharging of the wand. All of which you performed perfectly." Edlyn held up her hand. "Listen carefully, my dear. Spell-casting is not merely a repetition of words. You draw the energy into what you speak. You weave the power into your words."

Dally did not respond.

"I was Mistress of the hidden orb for thirty-two years. In all that time I have never seen an acolyte take to spells so naturally."

"I really am that, aren't I? An acolyte."

"That and far more besides. You are a wizard." Edlyn smiled in encouragement. "Now cast the first spell."

Dally found the spellwork to be utterly thrilling. She had asked the dragon for something similar to what their enemy had used upon the forest beasts. The image had come to her in the final series, how the resulting surprise and even fear might well work to their advantage. And keep them alive. Perhaps.

The spell's words condensed in her mind, in her very bones. Then they extended outward as she spoke. The wand's gemstone glowed with a blinding flash as she reached over and touched Nabu directly between his trusting golden eyes. It would hurt her the most if she wounded the dog, or if the dragon had been mistaken, or if she cast the spell incorrectly, or if it could not be applied to a wolfhound . . . Any number of things could go terribly wrong. But it would be her dog. She would endure the loss as punishment for her errors. If they survived.

In the end, though, all her concerns were for nothing. She finished the spell and stepped back, amazed by her own handiwork.

Nabu had grown to twice the size of a horse. His fur gleamed a bright blue, like flames seen through ice, save for the streak of white lightning along his spine. What was more, each breath sparked a puff of blue fire.

As she cast her spells over the other three dogs, the distant rumbling gradually became an earthquake. The screams and shouts were so loud now they could be heard echoing up and down the empty tunnel.

Connell surveyed the massive beasts and declared, "The sight gives me hope."

"It will be a genuine pleasure," Edlyn said, "to give our enemy a taste of his own medicine."

"I almost look forward to it," Connell said.

As though in response to his comment, there was a crashing sound from upstairs, followed by water cascading through the hole. They jumped back as the water fell harder and harder.

Edlyn cried, "Seal the opening!"

Connell was the first to react, creating a temporary block while Edlyn carved out segments of both walls and the floor, fitting the stones into place and melting the edges so that they melded together. Finally she said, "All right, release your spell and let's see if it holds."

Here and there the ceiling dripped. Edlyn decided, "Hardly my finest crafting. But it will do. And now we must hurry."

51

They walked down the tunnel a hundred paces. Two. Connell softly counted out the distance they covered. The dogs padded ahead so as not to huff blue fire upon the humans. Dally thought the city revealed its age much more clearly here belowground. The tunnel was carved from solid rock, a gigantic tube perhaps ten paces wide—a perfect square with slightly curved corners. The floor and walls held a subtle ridged pattern, as though the tunnel had been fashioned by some magical drill.

Finally Connell said, "According to Alembord, we should be directly under the treasury."

"Cast the dragon's second spell," Edlyn said. "Hurry."

The casting contained none of the fireworks of the first. But its impact upon Dally was even stronger. Her gemstone's force was reduced to a ruddy glow, yet it was enough. More than that. Dally cast the spell and stood entranced by the result.

"My dear," Edlyn said, "we have very little time."

The words were enough to bring the tunnel back into focus. "The vial is here," Dally said.

They looked at her, their expressions colored blue by the dogs' illumination. Both were severely intent.

Connell asked, "Are you sure?"

"I am. Yes."

"Describe what you feel," Edlyn said.

"I don't exactly know how to put it into words."

"Try," Connell pressed.

"I can sense her so clearly . . . It feels as though she is standing here beside me."

"Who?"

"The Lady Joelle." Dally smiled. "She's singing to me."

Edlyn asked, "What is she saying?"

"Just one word. Hyam. It's lovely."

Connell planted his hands upon his hips and stared at the distant ceiling. "We could cut at an angle. Carve stairs in the side wall."

"No," Dally said. She pointed to her right. "The vial holding Joelle's breath is right through there."

"Of course," Edlyn said. "The Milantians are suspected to be a race who prefer to live underground."

"There's more," Dally said. "I feel the current." She stomped her foot in the puddle. "Right here." She lifted her wand, closed her eyes, and shouted the spell with such force her echo filled the tunnel. Or so it seemed to her.

When she opened her eyes, her wand glowed more brightly than all the dogs together.

Edlyn reached out. "Give me that. Now recharge ours while I make us an opening."

52

Connell and Edlyn worked in tandem, melting their way through the side wall, while Dally recharged one wand after another. Dally insisted that the opening had to be large enough for the dogs to fit through comfortably. The rumbling overhead grew steadily louder. The occasional scream could be heard echoing faintly down the empty stone tunnel.

As she switched wands with Connell, Dally said, "We may be leaving in a hurry."

"Almost certainly," Connell agreed.

"I don't want the dogs to have to slow down and squeeze through," Dally said.

Edlyn extinguished her wand. "Stop, please." When Connell's wand went dark, she stepped forward and said, "Now that is interesting."

The tunnel's wall was reduced to slag and dust and steam where it touched the puddles. Before them was something else. Connell examined it carefully and declared, "New stone. Finely trimmed."

"And magically protected." Edlyn swept back the sleeves of her robe. "Give me that wand and recharge this one. All right. Stand back, everyone."

Connell and Dally retreated a dozen paces and drew the dogs with them. Edlyn called out words that caused the hair on Dally's neck to stand on end. The dogs all growled as one, illuminating the tunnel with more blue fire. Edlyn tapped her wand to the wall. A spiderweb of power grew between the stones, bright as summer lightning. Edlyn spoke again, and her wand became too bright to look at directly. She touched the wall a second time, a very delicate tap. The spiderwebs began to pulse, running in brilliant sequence from left to right. A third spell, and the wall blasted away.

Water spilled through the opening, rushing about Dally's ankles. Cries and shouts instantly became much clearer.

Then, in the distance, a bell began to toll. The sound was low. Mournful.

As solemn as an announcement of their doom.

53

Edlyn led them inside, raised her wand, and called out in a loud voice. All around them the torches sprang to life.

They stood inside a chamber that was the largest internal space Dally had ever seen, at least two hundred paces long and almost as wide. The distant ceiling appeared to be polished bedrock. The wall through which they had entered was new stone, but the floor had the same grooved ripples as the tunnel. To their left, perhaps thirty paces away, a vast stone staircase rose toward the city's clamor. Water spilled down the steps. And the alarm bell continued to sound.

"The time for subterfuge is past," Edlyn said.

"Speed is everything," Connell agreed.

Edlyn pointed to the staircase. "It appears that is our only entryway."

"Other than the way you just made, of course," Connell added. Not even the distant tumult or the alarm bell could completely extinguish his humor.

Edlyn scurried toward the stairwell. "I'll go stand guard. You two make all possible haste."

Dally took a firm hold of Nabu's shimmering fur. It felt somewhat the same as before the transformation, only now there was an electric bristle that sparked where she gripped him. She reached out to all the dogs and spoke the words aloud. "Stay with Edlyn. Obey her every word. If she commands you to attack, use everything you have to protect us. Stay safe. Remain alert to my signal. Come when I call. No matter how fierce the battle. Come when I call." She repeated the command three times, then released them with, "Now go."

All the while the great bell resonated through the chamber, inside Dally's bones. *Doom, doom, doom.* She was certain now the sound came from no forged instrument. It was magical in design, fashioned to freeze the invader with dread and woe.

Dally had no response save to raise her wand once more and repeat the spell. Hunting for Joelle's breath.

Instantly the bell's clamor was overlaid by a far sweeter sensation.

But there was a problem. A huge one.

Connell saw her dismay and demanded, "What's the matter?"

The cavern was set up like a gallery. Ornate shelves lined with every imaginable form of treasure stretched out before them. Rows of chests stacked like gaming chips leaned against the opposite wall. The nearest lanes contained hundreds of beautifully carved gemstone statues, many depicting animals Dally could not name. Barrels of ornamental swords with jewel-encrusted hilts. Hundreds of crowns. Thousands of necklaces and bracelets. Rows containing nothing but royal scepters. The treasuries of entire civilizations lost to time and defeat, all on secret display.

"Dally, talk to me!"

She swept out her arm, taking in the whole chamber. "The sense of Joelle's presence comes from *everywhere*!"

54

Doom, doom, doom.

Connell showed fear for the very first time. "What are you saying?"

Dally's second sweep of her arm was swifter, more frantic. "I hear Joelle's voice from a dozen different places. More."

"You *hear* her."

"Hear, smell, taste—none of these are the right words and yet they all are. That's not the *point*." She tried to stifle the shrill fear. "The echo resonates from a dozen different items. More. What do we *do*?"

Connell looked around, not at the treasure, but for an answer. "Is it a ruse?"

"I don't . . ."

"Camouflage? A masquerade?"

"I know what 'ruse' means. And no, that's not what I think. They all sound too *real*."

Connell's strength of resolve shone through his fear.

"There's only one answer, in that case. We take it all. Everything that resonates with you comes with us."

Water rushed down the stairs, so much that the floor was awash to ankle depth. Connell dumped over a barrel, scooped out the swords, and extracted a red leather sack that had been used as lining. "Here, take this." He moved to a tall, narrow crate holding six identical ceremonial staffs. "Symbols of a royal council at public gatherings," he explained, then dumped them on the floor and extracted a second leather sack.

"Wait. Take that sword with the big jewel in the pommel," Dally said, pointing to the staff by his feet. She rushed away, twenty paces on, to where a crown called to her. She stuffed it in the sack without pausing.

Each magnetic attraction was a light she could not see, a flame she didn't feel. She explained this to Connell as she directed him down to a mock wand of woven gold wire. She picked up two necklaces and a diadem from the next lane.

"Where to now?"

She pushed through the rising water. "Three shelves to your left, eye level, a scepter all by itself."

Connell hurried over, his footsteps splashing loudly. "What if the vial isn't here?"

"It's here." Of that she was certain. "Joelle is still singing to me."

Edlyn descended the stairs far enough to see them. "Can we withdraw?"

"Not yet!" Connell called back.

"They're coming!"

"Hold them off!"

Edlyn hesitated, clearly ready to argue. Then she scampered back out of sight.

Doom, doom, doom.

No matter where they went, how fast they struggled through the rising water, or how many treasures they dumped into their sacks, Joelle's voice continued to echo through the vast chamber, calling Dally on and on and on . . .

The first two sacks became so heavy they could not be lifted free of the rising water. So Connell hauled them back to the opening in the side wall, found two more, and returned. In the meantime Dally had scooped up three diadems, a ceremonial dagger, and a bird with four wings carved from a single ruby bigger than her two fists.

Connell took the prizes, handed her the empty sack, and gasped, "Do you see it yet?"

"No, no, no!" She was already running, or trying to, pointing two rows over as she did. "The sword with the violet jewel in the hilt! Take it!"

The sound of wizards doing battle echoed from the staircase. Sparks of power drifted over the ceiling and fell like electric snow to hiss and die in the water. But she did not hear the dogs, which Dally took as a good sign. Clearly Edlyn was holding them back as a final last-ditch surprise.

Dally was called to another goblet, this one golden and crystal, with a dragon carved into its side. Two more crowns, another necklace, then a dozen royal seals. She rounded the next corner . . .

And met Joelle.

"I have it!"

Connell rushed over. He gasped, "Are you sure?"

"I am certain."

"What's the matter now?"

"Nothing," she replied. "Everything is beautiful."

Of course, all Connell could see was an unadorned golden vial, two fingers in width and a bit longer than her hand. It was held within a stand of golden wire encrusted with some of the cavern's smallest jewels.

Dally picked it up and fought the urge to weep. She whispered, "Hello, dear friend."

Connell patted her shoulder, took the half-filled sack from her hands, and rushed away. "I'll go fetch Edlyn. Start moving the other sacks through the portal. We take the treasures, yes?"

"We take them all!" But Dally did not move. She felt immensely privileged. She stood there staring at the vial and knew with utter certainty that meeting Joelle like this had already enriched her life.

55

Dally carried her second sack back across the cavern, the water sloshing up to mid-calf now. She felt Joelle move alongside her. Singing of love and friendship and sunlight and hope . . .

Then Edlyn's shriek echoed down the stairwell. *"ATTACK!"*

The instant the wolfhounds bellowed, Dally entirely lost connection to Joelle. All four dogs roared. The water trembled violently, then washed over her knees as a massive blast of noise and force caused dozens of shelves to topple over.

Edlyn appeared. She needed both hands to keep her balance as she struggled down the stairs. Water rushed and pummeled her legs with each step.

Only when she was midway across the cavern did Dally realize the old woman was laughing. "I would not have missed that for the world."

Connell helped Edlyn through the opening, handed both women a sack, and then hefted the two heaviest himself. Staggering under the weight, he gasped, "Make a light."

Dally used her free hand to raise her wand. Water spilled through the portal, as did the sounds of magic and battle. They hurried away, fast as the heavy sacks allowed.

Connell was bent almost double under the weight of his load. "Who attacked you?" he asked Edlyn.

"Mages. Or rather, they would have, had Dally not thought to ask the dragon for that spell. Now they feast upon a taste of their own magic." Even burdened as she was, Edlyn still sounded merry. "What on earth are we carrying?"

"All the items that called to Dally," Connell replied.

Edlyn's good humor only increased. "In that case, each one is precious."

As they ran down the tunnel, Connell and Edlyn began a discussion that emerged in tight gasps. Connell wanted to call back the wolfhounds and seal the cavern's entry.

"Nonsense," Edlyn huffed. "Any wizard with a week's training would reopen the portal and fill the tunnel with flames."

"If there were mages at all," Connell said.

"Of course there were." She ran with remarkable ease for a woman of her age. "Don't be silly."

Dally hated putting so much space between herself and the wolfhounds. She had never tried to connect with four over such a distance. And of course there was their current magical state to consider. She had no idea if this would alter their ability to hear or erase their willingness to obey.

Even so, she knew Edlyn was right. Most likely Connell did as well.

They ran.

And through the distant portal came the sound of the wolfhounds' roars and the echoing refrain of the magical bell. Promising the direst of consequences.

Doom, doom, doom.

56

Connell saw it first. His every step faltered slightly now, and his hoarse breathing echoed loudly in the tunnel. Their footsteps sloshed and the dogs roared and still the bell sounded. But through his film of sweat-drenched hair, Connell cried, "Up ahead!"

Far in the distance glowed a faint light, one that should not have been there. But which ignited in all three of them enough strength to accelerate.

With each step the light grew stronger. Their footsteps lifted out of the water now, and they all grunted with each stride. The bags clinked loudly, and Dally's dug into her shoulder. Despite it all, she loved the run. She fought the fatigue that seeped through her bones, willing it to burn away in the race toward the light and safety.

A young voice called, "Who goes there?"

But they were too busy drawing enough breath to force their bodies forward. The light was strengthened until it illuminated both them and the torrential rain that blasted down through the hole in the tunnel ceiling.

"It's them!" The young lad's relief lifted his voice to where he sounded like a frightened little girl. "It's really them!"

They halted and let their sacks fall into the water by their feet. Dally's body ached now that she was able to stop. All three of them stood on trembling legs, gasping desperately for air. Connell faltered and would have gone down had the young mage not caught him.

Together they lumbered the last few paces, over to where rain-swept light spilled through a massive hole in the tunnel's roof. The opening at street level was fully fifty paces wide. The closer they came, the deeper the water grew and the harder the going. Up ahead of where they stood, beyond the rough-edged portal, a vast pile of rubble jammed the tunnel. Water seeped through in tiny driblets.

Connell halted where the rain fell straight into his face and stood there, the water streaking his grin, as he looked up and said, "Alembord!"

Half a dozen faces peered over the edge. The guards captain demanded, "What took you so long?"

Edlyn staggered over to Dally and said, "Call your dogs, my dear. Their work back there is done."

57

Alembord and his team had been very busy indeed.

Three neighboring structures had been torn apart and re-formed into the dam that now abutted the tower. There was no entrance to this tower, which Alembord had taken to suggest that it was not a normal tower at all. Rather, a solid stone structure had been erected here to maintain regularity. But the original designers had most likely decided they could not fashion a hollow edifice directly in front of the lake. The risk of it collapsing in spring floods was too great. This was important, Alembord explained, for it meant that the guards could not descend to ground level and fight them off.

Alembord's company had first demolished a massive building, the one closest to the tower. Myron and his most gifted acolyte burned a great hole into the tunnel, then the other three mages compressed the rubble, tighter and tighter, until it formed . . .

A giant stone cork. Which they jammed down tight, filling the tunnel entirely. Sealing off the water's flow for the first time in millennia.

Meanwhile, guards along the high ramparts had shouted and fired arrows, but neither had had any impact on the mage shields. So they had sent runners the five hundred paces in each direction, to where neighboring towers could grant them access to the streets. But long before reinforcements could arrive, the city's militia had far more urgent matters to contend with.

The dam blocking the tunnel had only been the beginning of Alembord's mischief.

The dammed river had to go somewhere. Not even a magically protected city wall could remain sealed against such a force. Especially in a deluge that strong, with the lake's water level rising at an alarming rate.

North of the city, the rain-swollen river continued to run into the lake. With nowhere else to go, the lake fed more and more water into the moat. The city's three portals became rivers themselves, flooding the markets and stables and streets. But not even that was enough to stem the flow.

Two of Alembord's mages hammered the tower and adjoining walls with a constant barrage of lightning bolts. Using this as cover, Alembord's remaining two wizards assaulted the tower's base. This had been the core of his strategy, fashioned with Edlyn the previous night—assuming Dally's image and the accompanying emotions were all correct, this mock tower formed the key to their escape.

But the wall was protected by centuries-old magic. Which meant . . .

The only logical answer was to attack the foundations.

They did not bother with subtleties like melting rock. As Edlyn had said, the time for subterfuge was long over. Once they had cleared the ramparts of defenders, Myron and his mages blasted through the cobblestones fronting the mock tower, down to where they breached the tunnel ceiling. Except these holes were steeply angled. Which meant they burrowed *under* the tower.

Myron was still cutting the first hole when the highly pressurized water finished the job for him.

The remaining earth and stonework blasted out, followed by a solid liquid cannon blast. The roar was immense, the power staggering. The geyser stripped away roofs and upper floors from buildings three streets away.

Myron and his company completed two more funnels, these angled even more sharply. And a fourth. A fifth. A sixth . . .

And then the tower crumbled.

Great cracks ripped apart the cobblestones. The earth groaned from the damage Alembord's company had wreaked. The cracks ran like stone veins up the city wall to either side of the ruined tower. Nature did battle with the wall's ancient magic. Nature won.

Despite the holes and the moat and the city's portals, the rain-swollen river and moat and lake all continued to rise. By the time that sixth hole opened, waves actually pushed against the wall's ramparts. With the foundations eaten away and the tons of water massed on its other side, the tower broke free of the wall and fell inward with a mighty sodden crash.

This was when Alembord's team became truly busy.

58

The one mage other than Myron who was able to recharge the wands was assigned that duty, while other wizards pulled down yet more neighboring structures, hurrying now, crushing and piling them into one monumental wedge. This new wall extended back around both sides of the opening, keeping the water from pouring back into the tunnel through which Dally and her company had to escape.

This wedge sheltered Dally and her company now. The massive wall of rock and rubble was magically protected, the wards held in place by a mage who only halted in her work long enough to turn and wave a greeting. To either side of their tight little island flowed the new overland river. The ruined tower formed a peak to their unnatural divide, around which two rushing currents invaded the capital city.

They clambered up to the top of their barrier and gawked at their handiwork. The flood filled one street after another, a massive torrent that rendered half of Port Royal under water.

The sound was monstrous, a sucking growl that rushed with constant fury through the ever-widening gap in the city wall. Dally reflected that the nicest part to all this clamor was how it erased her ability to hear the magical bell. But she knew it still resonated. She could feel it in her bones.

Alembord shouted to be heard over the din. "We must go!"

Under Edlyn's tutelage they began fashioning a bridge. Dally did not understand the magic being used, so she first reduced the dogs to their normal state, then helped the young female wizard in recharging the wands. The bridge was a rambling concoction of whatever was at hand—wood and condensed rubble and stonework and doors and window shutters. Stairs were fashioned, and together they began to climb. They clambered above the surging rivers, then higher still to where they could look down upon the ruined wall and drowning city.

At Edlyn's signal, the rearmost mages released their wards upon the wedge, and instantly the water's fury began eating away the barrier. They then heaved as much debris as they could manage into the hole, blocking the tunnel, keeping all the invading waters overland.

The bridge was little more than a thin stone line. Dally had not realized just how much she disliked heights until that moment. Her limbs were increasingly weak, her steps feeble. She kept her eyes pointed straight at the next step, which aided breathing somewhat. Every time she glanced up she watched as Edlyn continued to build the bridge out of nothing. Then through the rain she spotted their destination, a steep-sided ridge that formed the lake's natural outer boundary. Four waterfalls gushed down, feeding ever more water into the swollen body below.

And still the rain fell.

Though she no longer carried a sack, Dally's clothes weighed almost more than she could bear. Every step became a trial. She could now hear little else than her own gasping hunt for another breath.

Slowly, slowly, they approached the ridge. They were so high now the lake was lost to the storm. Dally was surrounded by the grey shroud of mist and the waterfalls' ceaseless thunder.

It was almost tempting to think of slipping over the edge. Giving up and falling away. The dragon's elixir had long since worn off. Dally battled against herself. She could think no further than the next step. And the next.

Then she realized the surface upon which she walked had changed. She smelled a grassy earthiness and cried aloud.

She did not fall so much as allow the ground to rise up and greet her.

59

The rain eased somewhat while they rested. The light strengthened a trace, and breaths came more naturally. Dally raised herself to a seated position and accepted Connell's spoonful of elixir. A broad pasture, several thousand paces wide, separated them from the forest. Far in the distance the river flowed, the channels swollen and the water surging angrily. Tall manors with empty eyes for windows rose beyond the waterways. Dally saw no sign of life, neither people nor animals. The only sound was of water. Falling from the sky, trickling over the rain-sodden earth, surging down the river's overflowing banks, tumbling over the precipice, striking the lake below.

Gradually her strength returned to where she was able to rise and stand under her own strength. But she dreaded the trek to come. Dally wished she could ask the Elves to travel this far from their glades. Bring the portal to them. Fashion it here, and then carry them away. To safety.

Edlyn walked over and said, "Try to charge your wand."

Dally shut her eyes, feeling the rain's chill fasten upon her joints and sinews, layering her clothes with unwanted weight. She searched down, down, then opened her eyes and confessed, "Sorry, Mistress. Nothing."

"No, nor I." Edlyn's smile was strained. "Well, never you mind. Safety is just up ahead."

"And soup," Connell said. With each step he sank in the muck to mid-calf. "And hot tea."

"Fresh-baked bread," Alembord said, slogging past them.

"A hot bath," Edlyn said. The old woman staggered and reached out for Dally's arm, almost bringing them both down. "Steaming water laced with an elixir for the joints. That's the ticket."

They slogged on for another hundred paces, fighting for every inch against the treacly mud.

Finally Edlyn gasped, "This won't do. This won't do at all."

They halted where they were. The mud was too deep to allow them to sit, so they simply stood there in the windless rain, gasping. Connell labored over to where Dally stood, gave her face one look, and wordlessly drew the jar of dragon's tears from his satchel. He filled the spoon and handed it over without speaking.

Dally interpreted his silence as, "I must look dreadful."

"While I look like a prince of the realm, no?" Connell's face was streaked with mud from where he had tried to clear the hair from his eyes. His eyes had retreated somewhat into his face, and his cheeks had turned craven from exhaustion. His gaze had a feverish gleam. "Should I try a mouthful, do you think?"

Dally's empty belly fought against the taste. She swallowed hard, again. Her hands trembled as she held them out to catch the rain. She drank, then managed, "Be my guest."

"Here's what we're going to do," Edlyn said. "Line up single file. One mage at a time will use what force we have to compress the earth. Ten paces only. The next mage in line will count the steps, then switch."

"I should have thought of that," Alembord said.

"Ten paces," Edlyn said. "I'll go first, then Myron. Dally, you—"

"I am taking my turn," she declared, though she had no idea how it would be possible.

Edlyn merely smiled. "Of course you will."

Despite their best efforts, it was hard going. The muck was very deep. By the sixth or seventh person in line, the earth released each footstep with a sucking reluctance.

"Aim left," Alembord gasped, pointing to where the first line of trees jutted out slightly. But to Dally it seemed that they were making almost no progress. She could still sense the magical bell back behind them, tolling their defeat.

They all slipped and fell at some point, which meant they were covered head to feet in slime. Alembord called a brief halt, not nearly long enough. They stood gasping in a frantic shared search for air. Despite the dose of elixir that still gummed her mouth, Dally felt her last vestige of strength draining away. She dared not look at how far they had to go.

And still the rain fell.

Then Connell cried, "The Elves have opened a portal!"

Alembord squinted against the mist and almost moaned, "Help is coming."

Edlyn mashed the way ahead as hard and dry as she could. "To the forest. Hurry."

Connell did not bother asking Dally if she needed help. He gripped her arm and supported far more of her weight than he really could manage. One of Alembord's guards who was not carrying treasure gripped her other side. Together they struggled on.

Then a voice behind them said, "I think that's quite far enough."

60

All around them rose a new wall. But one not made of thorns. Rather, this one was shaped from water.

Dally saw the rain veer in midair to be joined by all the groundwater. The liquid pulled away until she stood on a carpet of treacly muck.

This new wall was huge, far taller than the city ramparts, and utterly clear. Through it Dally saw the Elven warriors step through the portal and point in their direction. Then two of the Elves turned and called back inside. Instantly the tunnel vanished. To their immense credit, however, the Elven guards remained outside. They walked toward the wall with weapons drawn, calling angry words that Dally could not hear.

"Wave farewell to your little green friends," the enemy said. "While you still can."

The enemy sounded like a man. But he was fashioned from

water as well, just like the wall. Dally could see right through him. His voice sounded as though he gargled on the words.

"One of you will spend tonight on Birdcage Walk. I invite someone to volunteer. No?" The enemy spoke with amused patience. He took his time, savoring each liquid word. Enjoying their defeat. "Tomorrow you will all wish you had volunteered, I assure you. After a day and a night in my dungeons, you will all beg to be dangled from the wall. Do you hear me? Beg. Still no volunteers? Well, never mind."

Edlyn's wand held a mere glimmer of power. Myron's and Connell's and Dally's were even dimmer. Even so, Edlyn cried, "Mages, strike!"

They all did their best, knowing it was a futile attempt. But trying just the same.

Their combined force sent faint ripples across the enemy's surface. Nothing more.

"How noble. How useless." His laugh was dreadful. "You couldn't manage to recharge your wands here? Pity, that. Well, never mind."

Elven magic sparked on the liquid wall's opposite side. The flashes and explosions were made even more futile by their utter silence.

Dally sent out the dogs. Or tried to. Before they reached the enemy, their forelegs became encased in liquid chains. They fought and roared and would have done themselves damage had Dally not ordered them to be still.

"They will make such nice pets," the enemy told her. "Or perhaps they should go join my forest friends. See what pleasure comes from taking down the next family."

Dally's response was chopped off before it formed, because suddenly she could no longer find the air to scream.

"Now let me show you what *real* power feels like."

The water rose up and chained them. Dally was so frightened and furious and weary she did not actually realize at first why she could no longer speak. Water flowed snakelike across the earth and wove its way around each of them. Including the dogs. The liquid cage gripped her from feet to shoulders. She could see two of the dogs growling and straining against the force.

"Oh, come now. One of you must be willing to sing for me. No? Well, never—"

The enemy's final taunt was cut off. Because a dragon crashed down upon him.

61

The chains and barrier became water once more. The wall splashed down heavily, a rushing tide that swept Dally and several others off their feet. Not that they cared. Not in the least. For there before them stood a dragon made of the same crystallized water as the enemy who was no more.

The dragon watched her clamber back to her feet and chattered softly.

Dally flung herself at the dragon's liquid leg. It felt like she was trying to embrace a gemstone tree trunk.

The dragon's crystal eye swiveled around to observe her. Then he lifted his massive head and chattered his drumbeat speech. The power contained within his dragon spell filled Dally with a hint of the same force she experienced with each dose of the elixir. She breathed deep, drawing in as much as she could. Feeling it flow through her entire frame. Knowing with its arrival that they were truly safe.

It caused her to weep harder.

The dragon's spell caused a flat plank of water to rise up before them. The Elven warriors splashed their way through the muck just as the crystal plank became a set of double doors that were flung wide open. And through them stepped another liquid man.

Dally recognized this one and cried, "Jaffar!"

He took a long look at himself, then declared, "I am rendered speechless."

The dragon chattered long and low. Jaffar's own speech carried a trace of the gargled quality, but none of the menace. "Our ally greets the Lady Dahlrin. He wishes you to know that the enemy is not vanquished. Merely forced to retreat. His location has always been hidden. Why or how, our winged ally has no idea."

Dally realized the others waited for her to speak. She gathered herself, released one hand long enough to wipe her face, then said, "That is more than enough. Thank you so very, very much."

Jaffar continued to interpret the irregular speech. "He wishes to know if you managed to obtain the vial."

"It is in the sack. Along with many other treasures that called to me in the same voice."

"Guard them carefully. In time, their purpose should become clear."

"You don't know?"

"This is your quest. Not mine." The dragon hesitated and inspected the muddy and bedraggled company. "Though the ancient treaties still bind me, everything has changed now.

For we share a common enemy. One who corrupts the very fabric of magic. And there is also the matter of this new code I shared with you the first time we met."

"Unity," Dally said.

"The treaty barring me from entering human territories was set in place by the Ancients. And yet it is their power which imbued me with the message. Which caused me to call out for one of your kind to take heed."

Dally realized the dragon was trying to excuse his arrival. "Your coming saved us."

"I acknowledge this fact, Lady Dahlrin. Just as I accept that I am now involved in your struggle." He took a step back, causing Dally to release her hold. Then he extended his wings fully so that she viewed the raging rivers and the waterfall's steam and the clearing sky through his gigantic frame. "To know a dragon's name is to bind it to a fealty beyond the reach of human time. Lady Dahlrin, I am Tragan, king of the northern reaches and all who call it home."

Dally tried to respond. But at that moment she wept too hard to speak.

"When you have recovered, you and Jaffar will come to me. And Alembord. And the Lady Edlyn. A representative of the Elves. Hyam, if he is able. And any others of your company whom you care to include. Bryna must travel as well. You must inform the Ashanta high council that I insist upon her presence. We will speak of the future, and of the now."

Dally took several hard breaths, then managed, "Bryna's people will object."

"Those who oppose the unity are to sip water laced with Joelle's gift. Some will remain against bonding with outsiders. Most, however, will realize they allowed themselves to be tainted by the enemy's spell."

Edlyn exclaimed, "They *allowed* themselves?"

Tragan shifted his gaze. He did not speak, nor did he need to. His displeasure over Edlyn's interruption was clear enough.

Edlyn responded by dropping to her knees. He watched her for a time, then turned back to Dally and continued, "A drop of Joelle's life elixir will do for the entire Ashanta Assembly. As it will for you and your own company. Another for Hyam. And one more for those humans who have been tainted by this dark force. Hold the rest in case of another assault by our foe."

"I will do as you say." Dally stared up at the crystal head. "I did not allow the enemy to invade me."

"Not willingly. But you are the stranger. As is Hyam. You both have abilities that redefine the boundaries of human magic. And rendered you vulnerable to the enemy's poison. In fact, I would say reaching beyond the physical constraints refines you as more than human, young one. What is more, your greatest events come to you when you make contact with Elven magic. It renders you . . ."

She cried, "Tell me!"

"I have no clear notion," the dragon replied. "And in such a vital moment, I will not deal in supposition."

"Perhaps it is part of my quest," Dally said.

"Deliver Joelle's gift. Drink of it. Heal. When you are ready, child of the young race, come to me."

Tragan unfolded his massive wings once more. He extended his neck fully, roared to the sky . . .

And dissolved.

The portal vanished. Jaffar had time for a final salute, then he was gone as well.

62

The Ashanta were there to greet Hyam when he returned to his home village.

Bryna stood alongside Dally, sharing a smile that trembled with all the emotions it represented. Dally found it necessary to wipe her eyes, along with many of the others gathered there, but her emotions were her own. For her, the time held an almost overpowering sense of farewell. She knew more keenly than ever that this village was no longer hers to claim. She might return. She might dwell here for a night or a season. But it would always be as the outsider she had become.

By then most Ashanta had drunk of the elixir. One drop was all she had placed within the vast stone cauldron. The leader of their Assembly had drunk, and afterward he had stood there for a very long time, his face turned toward the sun, staring at nothing. Then he had ordered the Ashanta warriors to bring forward all those opposed to joining with their allies. Drag them, if necessary. Not all had retracted their demands for isolation. But most had. And now the Ashanta had another word for those who sought to hold themselves apart from their allies.

They were called the afflicted.

A new battle standard had been designed by the gathering of leaders. On a shimmering white background had been written one word in three tongues, Ashanta and human and Elven.

Unity.

The new standards lined the portal's entryway as Hyam arrived on a pallet carried by four allies. Meda gripped one handle, as did Connell and an Elven warrior and an Ashanta guard. Shona stood front and center to greet them. When the weakened emissary smiled her way, she knelt by his pallet and wept.

They waited while Hyam and the new queen exchanged words none could hear. There was no hurry now. The valley was perhaps the safest region in all the realm, rimmed as it was by Ashanta Seers and patrolled by Elven scouts and guarded by Shona's own troops. Across the valley from where they stood, a broad avenue was being carved into the forest. A similar highway was under construction through the forest fronting Falmouth Port. Many names were being tossed about by those who worked on the impossible road intended to draw together the queen's two enclaves, separated as they were by over a month's trek through hostile terrain and enemy-controlled fiefs. None of this mattered today. The road was started. It would be finished. Everyone gathered here was certain of that. It had become the symbol of a future. One built upon safety. And hope. And the enemy's eventual defeat.

Hyam was a mere shadow of his former self. His frame was gaunt, his limbs pale as old bones, his eyes feverish. But his smile was genuine. As was his greeting when they brought his pallet over to where Dally stood. "The first thing I heard upon awakening was my wife calling me back to life."

"I heard her as well, my lord," Dally said. "It was a joy to meet her."

"I'm glad you feel that way." His hand reached out and touched his wolfhound's head. "Then I opened my eyes, and there by my bed stood Dama."

Dally smiled at Hyam's new wolfhound. "I am so glad you two have bonded, my lord."

He continued to stroke the dog's head. "You really must call me Hyam. What are titles between friends?"

63

Elven warriors were spaced precisely along the forest trail that led from Honor village. The path had not been used in years and was almost lost in places, though Shona's troops had cut back the worst of the overgrowth. Hyam appeared to drift in and out of slumber, waking when the sunlight filtered down through the vast trees lining their way. Their company included a remarkable assortment of peoples—village elders from the length and breadth of Three Valleys, mages from Falmouth and the local Long Hall, Elves and Ashanta. Dally saw Jaffar wave to her from his position beside Ainya, the Elven queen. Dally looked forward to their first face-to-face conversation.

Just then, however, she was drawn around by Shona, who said, "Hyam asks that you join him now."

Their destination was an oval field that defied the forest's encroachment. It had not seen a human hand in years, but it still held the precise furrows of a careful plowing.

Hyam was seated on the pallet's edge, which rested alongside a small, bubbling spring and a farmer's shack. He reached out an arm to Dally and said, "Help me up."

He needed far more support than she could manage alone. Connell and Shona helped him cross the deep furrows. At a gesture from Hyam, Edlyn and Myron and Ainya all moved forward with them. Hyam's footsteps were little more than light contacts with the earth. He moved with his eyes tightly shut and his face turned to the sun.

He said, "Stop here." He breathed deeply, then said, "Move to the right. A bit farther. Now straight ahead two paces."

He stood there, eyes clenched shut, breathing in and out like a weakened bellows. Heaving the air in and out, tasting it with all his might. Then he turned to Shona and asked, "Do you feel it, old friend?"

"Who are you calling old?" Shona revealed a most delicate smile. She closed her eyes, concentrated, then replied, "Nothing."

"Connell?"

"What precisely are we after here?"

Hyam's response was to ask Edlyn, "My lady?"

"I have no idea what you are going on about."

He then turned to her. "Dally?"

She had already sensed something. But it unsettled her so much she had been reluctant to do more than stand there and observe the three men. "I'm not . . ."

Hyam's strained and exhausted features rearranged themselves into a smile of genuine approval. He said to the others, "Leave us, please."

64

When the others had retreated back across the oval field, Hyam said, "I want you to do something for me."

The power still coursed up through her feet, filling her with a sense of sheer potency, such that her voice trembled slightly. "What?"

"Mistress Edlyn has told me a little of your background, and the fear you harbor over your own potential." Hyam gave that a moment, then finished, "I want you to trust me."

"I'll . . . try."

"Excellent. I'm too weak to accomplish what is required, you see. And it probably requires one who can make the connection."

"Probably?"

His smile came more easily this time. "What we're going to try here has not been done in centuries. Longer."

She licked dry lips. "I don't understand."

Hyam eased himself down to sit upon the earth. "This land has been in my family for generations. No one could explain why the forest did not encroach. But every new season, we would arrive to find it as you see. The trees and the animals and even the weeds were kept back. And the land accepted our seeds almost greedily. My uncle taught me never to plant a handful, as is normal, for they would all grow and choke each other."

Dally dropped down beside him. The growth lay tight to the earth, the furrows still deep enough that she could cross her ankles and sit comfortably. "What caused such conditions?"

"Precisely. That is the question I awoke to. And you are here to supply the answer."

"How can you be certain?"

"Because," Hyam said, "I already see it in your hands."

"I don't understand. See what?"

"Stand up, Dally. Shut your eyes. Now extend yourself downward. Far as you can. Tell me what you sense."

She did as he instructed, though it terrified her. But here the fear was different from what she had known before. The *potential* alarmed her. "I don't think I can control it."

"But we're not after control, and you know it. What do we seek?"

She knew the answer as clearly as if it was scripted upon her closed eyes. "To channel it."

"Very good. Excellent, in fact. Now tell me what you sense."

"Rivers of power."

"And something more, yes?"

She felt his words press at her. Pushing her to reach down into the flowing power itself, seek with a confidence that was not her own, and discover, "There's something . . ."

"An orb."

She heard Hyam rise to his feet but felt no desire to open her eyes. She was bonded now, linked to something that seemed to sing in harmony to her heart's song. "What is . . ."

"You know. Don't you? It is yours." Hyam began retreating across the field. She knew because she heard his voice moving away. "It has been waiting thousands and thousands of years for you to come here and stand where you are. And call to it."

The sensation grew in harmony to Hyam's words. An accord that reached through the earth and rock below her feet, bonding her to the unseen orb.

"It is time for you to claim the orb, Dally," Hyam called with a strength that suggested he shared at least a trace of this same force. "Invite it upward. Bring it into . . ."

Hyam stopped speaking because she had already started the process. She did not know what to do, but knowledge was not required here. She asked, and the orb answered.

Dally lifted her hands. The sunlight seemed to coalesce and reach down through her body, deep into the earth, joining with the orb. She could see it now, the globe shining with such intensity she could observe its rise through the impossible depths.

Then the earth cracked and shifted and groaned and opened. Dally did not open her eyes. She was too intently focused upon the potency.

The orb fitted into her hands as though it had been fashioned to be gripped by her. And her fingers formed to hold it.

She lifted the orb over her head. She arched her back with the sheer exultation of feeling the flowing currents rise and course through her body. Fill the orb with the triumph of being brought into the here and now.

Dally opened her eyes.

Hyam stood to her right, laughing softly.

Before her stretched the assembled company of humans and Elves and Ashanta rimming the forest perimeter. Illuminated by a light that changed color as it streamed over them. Blue and gold and lavender and green and purple and orange and blue again.

Dally would have remained there for hours, days even. But Hyam walked back and touched the orb, drawing the power down to where it murmured softly in her mind.

Together they walked back to the company, where Hyam said to the Ashanta leader, "I would ask a boon."

"Anything, Emissary." The old man in his white robes gaped at the orb in Dally's hands. "Anything at all."

"Build me a cottage upon the point where the orb emerged," Hyam said. "A haven where I can sit and heal and return to life again."

The Ashanta bowed low. "It will be done as you have requested."

65

No one showed any interest in leaving the field that was to become Hyam's place of healing. The villagers and Elves brought together an impromptu feast. Shona settled down on Hyam's other side, then refused to accept the orb when Dally offered it. As did Edlyn and Connell and Myron in turn.

Hyam explained, "There is a joining process that is required between an orb and its mistress. Give yourself time to fully understand what this means."

Dally's entire frame shook from the first fragmented implication. "The orb's mistress?"

Ainya kept Hyam from needing to respond by stepping forward and gesturing to the orb. "Might I have that for a moment?"

When Hyam smiled and nodded, Dally handed it over. The Elven queen handed it to Vaytan, her aide. Dally decided there would be no better time to say, "Lady Shona, I would ask permission to offer fealty."

To her utter astonishment, Hyam said, "I think not."

"I agree," Edlyn said.

"Why ever not?" Dally looked from one face to the next. "You all have."

Connell settled down on Dally's other side. "What they mean is, your quest is not yet clear."

"I found the vial and brought it back," Dally pointed out.

"The vial, the vial." Hyam stretched out his legs. "I was lost in the darkness and the mists. Then they forced yet another dose between my lips and made me swallow. And Joelle spoke to me, calling me back." His smile was tinted with genuine sorrow. "I suppose I should thank you."

"You most certainly should," Trace said. "You scamp. To even question it is to scorn your beloved's gift."

Dally sensed Connell's closeness, a warmth that kindled the fires of her heart. She turned to him and found herself held by his gaze. He said softly, "May I have a word?"

She rose and followed him across the field, over to where a toolshed stood by a small pool. He stared intently at the water, as if seeking guidance or strength. "I don't know how to say what I feel I must."

Dally felt her heart hammer with such intensity she feared it might spring from her chest. Even so, she heard herself say calmly, "Speak the words, Connell. If you don't, I will."

He looked at her. "You too feel something between us?"

"Since the moment I first saw you."

He sighed. "All this time I feared, well . . ."

"I had my fears as well," Dally said. "You from a fine family, with a heritage that stretches back generations."

"You with incredible gifts," Connell replied. "And a role to play in all our futures."

"Only if someone with more wisdom and experience will offer a guiding hand."

Connell's gaze burned with an uncommon flame. "Say there will be a time for us."

"For us." She both whispered the words and sang them. "And soon."

They sat and stood, looking westward over the sunlit field. The shadows were lengthening now, the forest scents stronger in the hot air. Not a trace of wind touched them. Dally could still feel the flavor of Joelle's gift upon her tongue, though it had been over a month since she tasted the elixir. For an instant she felt as though she could see the beautiful woman hovering there in the light. Dally wiped her eyes, hoping for a clearer look. But all she saw was sunlight, and then the Elven queen standing before her, smiling and holding a most remarkable staff.

"My lady." Ainya held it out. "You may find this an easier way to carry your orb."

The staff was as long as she was tall. Its entire polished length was inscribed with letters that looked as though they had grown into the wood. Dally accepted it, hefted it, and exclaimed, "It weighs nothing!"

"Here, watch what I do and how I speak." Ainya chanted a

brief plainsong, and the roots gripping the orb slipped back. She lifted the jewel, then settled it into position and chanted once more, regrowing the roots. "Now you try."

As with all the other spells she had learned, Dally felt as though she did not speak the words but rather greeted them as they emerged from somewhere deep inside. All the mages stared at her in astonishment—all save Edlyn, whose smile competed with the Elven queen's for brilliance.

Ainya said, "When you are ready, you must come and reside with my clan and learn our tongue."

Dally quailed at the prospect of being surrounded by Elven magic and all that portended. But all she said was, "Thank you, Majesty."

Bryna said, "First she will come as a guest of our people. We have much to discuss, this far-seeing human and I."

Hyam said, "It is time for you to take the next step of bonding with your orb. Move away from us and speak a spell, and utter it using the orb as your focal point."

"Here, first give me your wand," Connell said. As she moved in close he murmured, "Do us all the great favor of aiming your force away from us, yes?"

As Dally crossed the field, alone this time, she felt as though the orb spoke with her.

Someone called out, "Is everything all right?"

She did not reply. She could not even say who had spoken. But she did not mind the interruption. In fact, their concern carried a welcome reassurance.

She was not exactly certain what was to happen or what she was to do, and then she was. It was that simple. She simply directed her unspoken question to the orb, which was far more than a vessel of power, she realized. It carried the ability to assist, to clarify, to instruct. The bonding was a process that reached in two directions. Dally now moved in keeping with her quest. She had never felt so vividly the link between her direction and who she was, this woman who had remained hidden inside the garden shed for years of lonely yearnings. Now she was alone once more, and yet it was by her own free will. Part of this chrysalis process. Growing her wings. Finding the power to lift free from the earth.

Dally shut her eyes and lifted the staff. The orb gleamed so strongly it blazed through her eyelids, illuminating the reaches where she sought to travel.

She would never again need to find an Elven portal to touch the power required to far-see. Nor would she ever again fear the action. Of that she was utterly certain.

Everything was changed now. She knew that as she accepted the orb's gift of Elven forces and Ashanta far-seeing. Dally allowed herself to be swept away.

She had no idea how long she stood there. Only that when she returned, the forest shadows stretched across the oval field. She walked back to where the company waited, her way illuminated by the orb's glow. She stood there, studying the myriad faces who had come to mean so much to her.

Finally she said to Edlyn, "I know the answer to the question you continue to ponder."

Edlyn smiled so tightly her eyes filmed over. "Speak then, my dear."

"You want to know why the enemy came to Three Valleys."

"It could not be for this orb," Edlyn said. "Otherwise he would already have it in his possession."

"And yet he hunted such an orb," Dally said. "Whose force was so strong he remained blinded by it. Unable to realize that yet another was here. Within his grasp."

Connell said, "There is another orb in the Three Valleys?"

"No," Dally replied.

Hyam smiled at her then. It was more than mere approval. He looked at her as . . .

An ally.

Dally said, "There are three. One in the valley's heart. And two more together. Forged into one mightier than all the others. Where the five currents of power flow . . ."

Bryna exclaimed, "By our settlement?"

"Just outside your boundary stones, beneath the headlands." Dally turned to Shona. "Where you will build your palace."

Thomas Locke is a pseudonym for **Davis Bunn**, an award-winning novelist with worldwide sales of seven million copies in twenty languages. Davis divides his time between Oxford and Florida and holds a lifelong passion for speculative stories. He is the author of *Emissary* and *Merchant of Alyss* in the Legends of the Realm series, as well as *Fault Lines*, *Trial Run*, and *Flash Point* in the Fault Lines series. Learn more at www.tlocke.com.

EXPLORE THE
WORLD OF

THOMAS LOCKE

Subscribe to the Blog

Find Previews of
Upcoming Releases

And More

tlocke.com